Restoration

SONJA GAMBRELL

Cover Design by Angela Haddon
angelahaddon.com

Edited by Book Helpline
bookhelpline.com

Print Format by The Book Khaleesi
www.thebookkhaleesi.com

Chapter One

M r. Corbin," Gaston repeated for the third time in a row. His decidedly unresponsive patient kept his focus on the sketch pad he drew on. "Henry." Gaston cleared his throat. Ocean eyes flicked up at him. He had finally used the correct name. "You just got your sketching privileges back," Gaston reminded Henry. "Do you really want them revoked again so soon?"

Henry went back to his sketch. "What I want doesn't matter." He brushed sandy bangs off of his forehead. "You're going to do whatever suits you. Go ahead and punish me if you want, Dr. Bell."

Gaston set his pen down on top of his notes. "I'm not out to get you. You're the one punishing yourself," the doctor said. He leaned forward. Henry refused to make a reciprocal move. "The longer you refuse to participate in therapy, the farther away you push recovery," Gaston added.

Recovery. Henry rolled his eyes and continued drawing. He was sure that was the last thing the good doctor was interested in. Even if there were anything wrong with him.

And there wasn't. Dr. Bell was getting paid enough to keep him in there.

The face of a woman took shape under his pencil. Nearly five years had passed since Henry had laid eyes on her, but he remembered every detail very clearly: the shape of her nose, the exact shade of turquoise her eyes were, the curve of her lips. As he shaded them in, he allowed his mind to wander. The doctor's voice was soon lost. Henry had long ago learned to tune out that noise. He lost himself in flashes of the brunette he drew. He could still see how her hair bounced as she bobbed around his studio to one of those rock songs she liked so much. She turned around as one flash bled into the next. Now in an evening gown, she sauntered up to him at his easel and smiled at him over the canvas he was working on. The project was a blur to him now like many of his other paintings. It soon shifted places in his mind's eye and was hung on a gallery wall with several of his other paintings. The same brunette was by his side, their fingers entwined. Her excitement vibrated through her hand as she tugged him along. He could almost hear her urging him to show her more of his work.

Henry was yanked back into the doctor's office as Gaston snatched the sketch pad away.

"It's not finished!" Henry grabbed the pad and pulled it back. He promptly turned the cover through the spirals holding the pad together and placed it over his work.

"You were daydreaming again," the doctor charged.

Henry tapped the pencil against the edge of the paper.

"About her?" Gaston challenged.

Henry pressed his lips together with a slight flick of his head. Dr. Bell got an affirmative answer from Henry's body language.

"How many times is that this week?" Gaston inquired.

Henry shrugged. He wasn't keeping count.

Seeing this route of discussion was going nowhere, Dr. Bell decided to steer toward the original topic. "Is there some reason you don't want me to see what you've drawn?" He leaned against his desk.

"How about privacy? I said it's not done," Henry snapped. "There are very few people I share my unfinished work with."

"And your Elizabeth is one of them?" Gaston leaned against his desk.

Henry cast his eyes down to the sketch pad. "You don't listen to me so why should I listen to you?" Henry rejoined.

"What makes you say I'm not listening?" Dr. Bell questioned.

"First off, my name." Henry set his shoulders.

"Henry Corbin," Gaston said.

"Angevin. Henry Angevin, why is that so difficult to grasp?" Henry slid his pencil into the spiral of the pad.

"Your half-brother is pretty convincing," Dr. Bell replied.

"He is not my brother," Henry spat. His lip curled back in disgust. "Haven't you noticed Arthur and I don't look anything alike?" Henry lifted his hands palm side up.

Gaston justified the discrepancy. "Half-siblings don't necessarily share a resemblance."

"To the best of my knowledge, I am not related to any Corbins," Henry asserted.

"To the best of your knowledge?" Dr. Bell raised an eyebrow.

"I have no clue who my father is," Henry acknowledged, "But my mom commented on how much I looked like him on several occasions."

"She knew who he was, but never told you?" Gaston questioned.

"I asked her once." Henry hung his head. "It made her cry so I never asked again."

"Your mother —" Gaston began.

"Grace Angevin," Henry clarified.

"It sounds like you love her deeply," Dr. Bell remarked. "Maybe if you showed some progress she could come for a visit."

"She died when I was thirteen," Henry replied.

"I'm sorry for your loss." Gaston bowed his head.

"You finally believe something," Henry muttered under his breath.

"You understand that someone with your history of delusions and obsessive tendencies —" Dr. Bell began.

Henry cut the shrink off. "I'm delusional and obsessive now."

"You draw the same woman over and over again," Gaston said. "What does that type of behavior say to you?"

"Have you ever heard of character studies?" Henry shot back. Normally he'd bite his tongue, but not today. Henry stretched his arms up and to the side. He rested his head in his hands back into the tall armchair in which he sat. "I did a ton of them at SoCal before I graduated."

"It's more than that, and I think you know it," Gaston charged.

"Elizabeth is my muse," Henry asserted.

"Liz Corbin?" Dr. Bell leaned against his desk.

"Elizabeth *Harper*," Henry corrected him. Elizabeth never changed her name. Not even to make that mock marriage look real. Gaston took note of the irritation in his tone. "She has a son named Richard. If you'd bothered to check, you would find a very blue-eyed, very blond boy," Henry challenged. The implications hung heavy in the air, though they went unspoken. A silent standoff ensued and lasted for several minutes.

"You need to help yourself," Gaston coaxed.

"I think I'd like to go back to my cell now." Henry smiled forcefully.

"This isn't a prison," Dr. Bell insisted.

Henry snorted at the remark. He pushed himself up out of the seat.

Gaston held his hand out. "Forgetting something?"

Henry hooked an arm around the sketch pad. He clutched it to his chest and turned around to exit the office. "I can walk myself out." Henry went for the door. He stepped out to be met by an orderly. "Max," Henry acknowledged with a tip of his head.

"Done already today, Henry?" the orderly rejoined. Henry didn't answer instead his gaze fixed on someone behind the orderly. Arthur Corbin stood there, gray eyes looking down his nose at Henry. Henry set his jaw. He puffed up to his full height. Knowing this could end badly, the orderly grabbed Henry by his shoulder. "Let's move along." The orderly began to force Henry down the hallway.

Henry fought against the muscled man to turn around. "You know I don't belong here!" he shouted at Arthur. Once they turned a corner, Henry stopped struggling. It wasn't as if he wanted more time with Arthur, no matter how good it would feel to pound on him.

"Mr. Corbin, why don't we talk in my office?" Dr. Bell

motioned for him to follow. Arthur gave a mournful look in the direction Henry had departed and then marched into the office.

"I guess there has been no progress." Arthur sat down in the chair in front of the desk.

"There's only so much that can be done if your brother is not willing to engage in therapy," Gaston admitted. "Maybe if she could come in and talk to him, maybe this could give him the push he needs to—"

Arthur cut him off with a look. "I think my wife has been put through enough." He crossed his arms over his chest. "It's time I prioritize her over him."

Dr. Bell switched tactics. "He mentioned a boy today—Richard. What can you tell me about him?"

"Richard? Henry had a son he named Richard," Arthur offered.

"Where is he?" Gaston inquired.

"He died of SIDs when he was a month old," Arthur answered.

"And you are just telling me this now?" Dr. Bell pinched the bridge of his nose.

"I told his first doctor," Arthur replied. "It's in his file somewhere. I thought you were supposed to read those things."

"Will took a lot of his files when he left. I've had to work on Henry's case from scratch." Dr. Bell blew out a breath.

Arthur frowned. "I will give him a call and get it over to you."

"What about the baby's mother? Maybe she can help," Gaston said.

"She skipped not too long after the baby died. We haven't

heard from her since." Arthur shrugged.

"Is it possible for you to track her down?" Dr. Bell requested.

"It might take some time, but I will see what I can do," Arthur said.

"Call me and we'll set up something once you find her," Gaston replied.

"If she's willing to come in, I'll let you know," Arthur cautioned.

"Thank you."

Arthur straightened his suit jacket. "Now is that all?" he asked dismissively.

"Yes, that's your report," Dr. Bell answered. Arthur and he stood. "Thank you for your time." Gaston reached over and shook Arthur's hand. "Are you going to visit with Henry?"

Arthur cringed. "I think it's best if I skip that today. He seemed ready to rip my head off."

Gaston tipped his head. "He's been in a contentious mood."

"Maybe I'll drop by another time." Arthur exited the office.

<hr />

Elizabeth grabbed her phone as quickly as she could to keep the ring from waking her young son. "Hello," she answered.

"Hey, Liz, just thought I'd check in before heading out," Oliver said.

"What are you up to today?" Elizabeth asked.

"Nothing interesting—some prep-work research at some

psychiatric hospital. My agent set it up," he said.

She snickered. "You certainly commit to your roles."

"How are the two of you doing?" he inquired.

"We're fine." Elizabeth smiled. "Richard is still solidly asleep." The ease in her voice sounded genuine this time. "I think playing with Orlando and Ophelia last night wore him out," she added.

"Good," Oliver replied. "How are his nightmares?"

"Decreasing. Not being around Arthur has helped a lot," Elizabeth reported. The time living in the penthouse was doing wonders for both her and her son.

He knew everyone else in her life was too afraid of Duncan to stand up to him.

"Are you going to need someone to watch Richard during your shoot next week?" Oliver asked.

"Calvin likes him, so he'll be fine tagging along," Elizabeth declined, rather loathe to let Richard out of her sight for too long. "Have you heard anything from Robinson?" Elizabeth inquired.

He frowned. "I'm afraid not. We were supposed to meet yesterday, but he didn't show."

"Father probably found him and paid him off."

"That would make what? The third investigator in a row?" Oliver rubbed the back of his neck.

"This year," Elizabeth replied.

"OK, well, we need to figure out another avenue to explore, 'cause this one isn't working," he pronounced.

"It's been nearly five years with no news." She fingered the hem of her pajamas. Her eyes drifted down to watch her hands. Elizabeth began to ramble her fears. "What if Arthur had Henry killed then? The men that dragged him away had guns."

"You can't let yourself think like that, Liz," Oliver admonished gently. "Henry is out there somewhere. Five hours, five days, five months, five years, whatever; we are going to find him and bring him home."

Elizabeth cleared her throat. "Thanks, I needed that." An almost inaudible coo came from Richard's room. From her vantage point in her sitting area, she saw Richard's bedding move. "I gotta go. The little one is waking up." Elizabeth got to her feet.

"Call me if you need anything," Oliver urged.

"You've already done so much for us," she replied.

"What kind of friend would I be if I didn't take care of Henry's girl and son for him?" Oliver deflected. "Talk at ya later, Liz."

"Bye." Elizabeth hung up.

She left her room and headed for Richard's. Elizabeth crossed over to the bed. She sat down next to the groggy little boy. She beamed. "Good morning, angel."

Richard rubbed his eyes and sat up. "Morning, Mama." He hugged her and wouldn't let go.

"You want to cuddle, don't you?" Elizabeth said.

"Mmm hmm," Richard replied. She smirked. Her son woke slowly like his father.

Elizabeth scooped him up. "All right, we'll go cuddle on the couch."

Max returned his charge to his room in another wing of the

asylum. "I'll be back to get you for lunch," the orderly promised.

Henry flopped down on the bed. He turned over. It creaked with his movement. To pass time, Henry studied his room's ceiling. He knew every little imperfection. The silence was broken when someone unlocked the door to Henry's room and opened it. He closed his eyes and prayed it wasn't who he thought it was. Henry pushed himself to a seated position. He found a brown-eyed nurse had entered. The resident minx was the lesser of two evils, he supposed, but not by much.

She pulled a hair tie up from her wrist and used it to gather her platinum hair back into a ponytail. "I just came by to see if you needed anything." Her eyes darted about the sparse room. There was nothing much for her to straighten up.

"Other than busting out of here, I don't need a thing." Henry crossed his arms over his chest.

"You know I can't help with that." She smirked. "I'd be happy to help with anything else." She sashayed toward him.

"Leave me alone, Serena." He pinched the bridge of his nose.

"I take it your session didn't go well," Serena replied as if she hadn't heard him.

"I'm not in the mood for company." He threw his head back. It hit against the wall.

Serena plopped down beside him on the mattress. He picked himself up and moved further onto his side of the bed.

"You dropped this." She reached behind her to retrieve his sketch pad and pencil. Serena offered them up to him. Henry eyed her warily. "Take it," she urged. "It's yours until your chart says you can't have it anymore."

"Thank you," he said watching the sketch pad as Serena

handed it over. Her shoulders fell. Not quite the excited reaction she had hoped for. In his time here she had never once seen him happy.

He turned the cover up and onto a new page. Serena sat by for a moment and watched Henry work. The outline of a woman quickly appeared. Serena's shoulders dropped. It was probably the same woman he had drawn over and over during his stay. Upon his refinement Serena could tell the jawline wasn't as angled, the chin rounder. This was someone else. She was sitting too with something—no, someone, a child on her lap.

"Boy or a girl?" Serena queried.

Henry shifted so she could no longer see the page. "Me," he said succinctly.

"How adorable, you and your mom." She beamed. Henry scowled at her over the sketch pad. His objection went ignored. "You're very talented," Serena continued. "Your drawings, they remind me of black-and-white photographs."

Maybe if he talked Serena would go away. "I prefer paints," Henry remarked. "Ollie always said I spent way too much time with my nose in a canvas."

"Have you heard from your friend lately?" she asked. "Oliver, I mean. As close as you say the two of you were, I'm surprised he hasn't come to visit you by now."

"I've told you. He doesn't know where I am," he said. Henry's chest sank. No one who cared about him knew where he was. Serena could tell she had hit a nerve.

"Now that we've talked, can I have a few minutes alone?" he requested.

"All right." She pushed off the bed. Serena headed for the door but only got a few steps out before turning around. "If

11

you ever need a new subject, I'm available." Serena batted her eyelashes at Henry.

He kept his face and voice neutral. "Aren't two reprimands for flirting with patients enough for this month?" he taunted.

"Yeah, I'm just saying if you get bored—" she began.

"I already have a muse," he declined coolly.

Serena's face turned red and not from embarrassment. She glared at Henry. "Serves you right if you were stuck here another five years," Serena snapped. She spun on her heels and stormed out of the room.

Once the door stopped reverberating, silence returned to the room. Silence, but not peace. Henry straightened out his legs. His sketch pad dropped into his lap. Another five years? He didn't see himself lasting much longer. Something had to give and soon.

Chapter Two

T he sun was still beating down. The heat made it almost unbearable to be in the courtyard. Henry kept mostly to himself as was his habit on these rare days when he was allowed outside. He sketched in a corner.

"How many patients does a doctor here typically treat?" He had to be hearing things. "Oliver?"

There was a light at the end of the tunnel after all, that is, if he could catch his friend's eye. "Ollie!" Henry yelled at the top of his lungs.

"Calm down," an orderly commanded. That just made Henry try harder. Jumping up in the air he waved. The orderly stepped in, but Henry had already caught Oliver's attention.

Oliver made a beeline for his friend. "Henry!" he called.

The friends embraced heartily.

"Henry, are you a sight for sore eyes!" Oliver proclaimed.

"For your own safety, Mr. Tate, step away from the patients." The man giving Oliver the tour put his hands on his hips and tried to catch his breath.

"He won't hurt me," Oliver responded to the shrink.

"And how do you know that for sure?" the tour leader replied.

"Because I went to high school with this guy," Oliver replied. "This is Henry Angevin, my best friend."

Henry nodded profusely. "For a minute there, I was afraid you wouldn't recognize me," he admitted.

"I'd know you anywhere—even behind that ferret on your face," Oliver teased with a smile.

Henry rubbed his chin. "They banned me from razors for the past few months."

"Don't worry about it. We're going to get you home," Oliver promised. "Liz has been worried sick about you."

"How is Elizabeth?" Henry inquired.

Oliver's shoulders fell. "You two have a lot to talk about."

"And Richard?" Henry made sure to catch Oliver's brown eyes.

"He's OK," Oliver assured the father. "And he'll be doing much better once we get you back in his life."

"What the hell are you doing here?" Henry inquired.

"I'm doing research for my next role," Oliver explained.

Henry chuckled. "Of course." His face suddenly fell. "You're not playing a shrink, are you?" he inquired.

"Who's in charge here?" Oliver demanded.

"Dr. Keller."

"I want to speak with him now," Oliver replied.

"He's making rounds at the moment," the guide said.

"I said now," Oliver commanded.

"I'll take you to his office," the tour guide offered.

"Henry is coming with me," Oliver asserted. "I am not leaving here without you." Oliver squeezed his friend's forearm.

They were shown into the director's office.

"I'll page, Dr. Keller. There will be an orderly on the door if you need anything at all." He exited, making sure to leave the door open.

Oliver looked over his shoulder through the door at the orderly. They would have to watch what they said.

"You hanging in there?" Oliver asked.

Henry blew out a breath. "Barely. I don't know what I would have done if you hadn't shown up today."

An older gentleman in a white lab coat came in. He shook both of their hands. He introduced himself as Dr. Keller.

"The only Henry we have an active file for is a Henry Corbin." Dr. Keller sat in his chair. The other men took that as a cue to sit as well.

"Well, that is not his name," Oliver asserted. "Henry was taken just under five years ago."

Dr. Keller inspected the file in front of him. In a few months, it would be Henry's fifth anniversary there. "His arrival was before my time," Dr. Keller said.

"His girlfriend and I have been looking for him all that time," Oliver added.

There was hardly any time for the information to sink in when Gaston and Serena came in together.

"You paged me, Dr. Keller," Gaston said.

"There is an issue with one of your patients," Dr. Keller replied. Dr. Keller motioned toward the newcomers. "This is Dr. Bell and Nurse Wilson. He is in charge of Henry's treatment."

Oliver felt Henry immediately bristle at their presence and stood, placing himself in front of his friend like a shield. "I am Oliver Tate," the actor introduced himself.

"I've seen a few of your movies." Gaston reached out his hand to shake Oliver's.

Oliver kept his hands at his side and angled back. "Henry here is my best friend," he began. "I want him released."

Gaston brought his hand back down. "I am not comfortable with that."

"I can guarantee a great big public stink from both me and Liz Harper if he is not immediately released," Oliver asserted.

"Liz Harper—that name sounds familiar," Dr. Keller replied. "She's a model or something?"

"Yes, a pretty high-profile one," Oliver answered.

"Liz as in Elizabeth —?" Gaston began.

"Yes, my Elizabeth," Henry cut him off.

The two exchanged glares before Gaston turned his attention back to Oliver. "His half-brother brought him in for a reason," Dr. Bell asserted.

Oliver laughed. "*I* am the closest thing Henry has to a brother."

Henry nodded.

"With all due respect, Mr. Tate—" Gaston started.

"You got duped, Dr. Bell." Oliver put his hands on his hips. He was not backing down.

"Mr. Corbin seems very concerned for his wife," Gaston countered.

"Arthur sold you some sort of stalker story," Oliver scoffed.

"And why would he do that?" Dr. Keller inquired.

"To stop me from claiming my child," Henry blurted out. Oliver's jaw dropped. They'd never talked about Richard's paternity this openly with strangers before. He recovered quickly. "Elizabeth and I have a son together," Henry explained.

"The two of you were having an affair?" Dr. Keller raised an eyebrow.

Henry scowled. "It's more complicated than I care to get into at the moment."

Dr. Keller watched the younger man slink further into the seat. He was beginning to believe his doctors had stepped right into the middle of a love triangle.

"I would never hurt Elizabeth. My kid needs his mother," Henry insisted.

"Give me a phone and I'll get Liz herself down here," Oliver said.

"Use mine." Dr. Keller lifted his receiver and handed it to Oliver.

Oliver dialed her number and prayed she was home. It only rang a couple of times before she answered.

"Hello?"

"I found him, Liz," Oliver reported.

"What?" Elizabeth questioned.

"Henry is sitting right next to me," Oliver clarified. "I'm looking right at him."

"Let me talk to him," she requested. Elizabeth had to hear Henry's voice for herself.

Oliver held the phone out for Henry. "She wants to talk to you."

Henry swallowed. He looked at the phone wide-eyed but took it. "Elizabeth?" Henry breathed.

"Is it really you?" her voice cracked.

"It's me," he replied.

"Give me the address, and I will be there as fast as I can," Elizabeth requested.

"I don't even know the name of this place," Henry said.

"Wonder Ridge or something like that." Oliver shrugged. He hadn't paid that much attention when his agent set up the tour. They looked to Dr. Keller, and he gave them the information. Henry relayed it to Elizabeth.

"I am on my way, baby," she crooned.

"Drive safe. Don't go too fast," Henry urged.

"I'll be careful," Elizabeth promised before reluctantly hanging up.

"She's coming," Henry said, handing back the phone.

———

Small talk filled the next hour as Oliver tried to get Henry's mind off of the time. "Miranda and I had another kid. I have a daughter now," Oliver revealed.

"No way." Henry clasped Oliver on the shoulder. "Congratulations."

"Ophelia." Oliver brought out his wallet and took out a brag picture. He showed it to Henry.

"She's beautiful. Gets a lot of her looks from her dad," Henry remarked.

"Karma is going to get me back when she grows up." Oliver raked his hand through his dark brown hair. Henry laughed. "It's already started with your boy. Whenever Ricky's over, he follows Ophelia everywhere." Oliver grinned. "I think he has a puppy crush on her."

Elizabeth burst through the door. Henry stood as she entered. Her hazel eyes locked on the man she had been searching for. Elizabeth beamed. "Henry."

RESTORATION

Henry was not ready for the air that rushed into his lungs. For the first time in forever, Henry felt solid again. He had been living like a ghost for so long. The feeling of the ground under his feet was something he'd have to readjust to. The light behind his eyes returned. Henry smiled as if he had never smiled before.

She ran to Henry, stopping herself by grabbing hold of his neck. Elizabeth rained kisses all over Henry's face, stopping short of his mouth. He rested his forehead against hers. She pressed her lips together. Elizabeth wrapped her arms around him. Henry reciprocated the gesture.

Gaston had to do a double-take. She looked exactly like Henry's drawings. Gaston cleared his throat.

Elizabeth glared at him for breaking the moment. They needed to get on with sorting things out.

"Are you all right, Mrs. Corbin?" Gaston questioned.

"Ms. Harper," Elizabeth corrected him. "And I am better than all right. Why wouldn't I be all right?"

Gaston straightened his shoulders.

"After that reaction, you still think she's afraid of me?" Henry questioned incredulously.

"Henry doesn't scare me." Elizabeth snuggled into Henry's chest to prove the point.

Henry tightened his embrace around Elizabeth. "I have never been afraid of him," she added.

Serena nearly gagged at the display. She crossed her arms over her chest.

The couple didn't seem to notice. Elizabeth looked up at Henry. He drew his hands up and down her arms. His fingertips ran over a raised line and then another. Henry frowned. Those shouldn't be there. He craned down and lifted up the loose sleeve to get a better look. Scars from cuts had formed. They looked fairly recent.

"What's this?" Henry locked eyes with Elizabeth. Her hazel orbs were darker somehow, sadder.

"A lot has happened since your abduction," she said softly.

"Did Arthur do this to you?" he questioned matching her volume.

Elizabeth felt Henry reading her. He knew her so well. She licked her lips. "Yes," Elizabeth answered. Henry pressed his tongue to the roof of his mouth. Rage rumbled in his stomach.

"How did you—?" Elizabeth asked.
"I know your body," he replied with a gruff tone that fell just this side of possessive.

Dr. Keller reached over his desk and offered his hand to shake Elizabeth's hand.

"Ms. Harper, I'm Dr. Keller. This is Dr. Bell."

"I want Henry released immediately and all of his artwork from his time here," Elizabeth demanded.

"Shouldn't we be talking with our lawyers?" Gaston looked to Dr. Keller.

Elizabeth cocked her head and crossed her arms over her chest. "You do not want to involve lawyers." She raised a perfectly arched eyebrow. "If you take it there, then not only will I shut this place down, I will have the license of every medical professional that works here!"

"I am sure we can work things out without going to such extremes, Ms. Harper," Dr. Keller intervened.

"For your sakes, I hope so. I can be my father's daughter," Elizabeth said. No one was going to stop her from getting Henry out of there.

"Your father?" Dr. Keller replied.

"Duncan Harper, Hollywood power player with enough connections and an ego to match," she clarified. "He's probably the man who's been bankrolling this."

"Is there any documentation you can show me to confirm Mr. Angevin's Identity?" Dr. Keller asked.

"I have his birth certificate here." Elizabeth pulled it out of her purse with one hand, keeping the other on Henry. She unfolded it for Dr. Keller. "And there is his driver's license. The picture is old, but it's him."

Serena looked over the things on the desk as Dr. Keller spread the documents in front of him. "Where did you get these?" the nurse questioned.

"Who the hell are you?" Elizabeth narrowed her eyes on the blonde. She seemed a bit out of place there.

"Serena Wilson. I'm one of the main nurses in Henry's unit." Serena held her head high.

"And you are here because?" Elizabeth deliberately furrowed her brow.

"I brought Henry's sketch pad." Serena held up the book.

"Thank you." Elizabeth held out her hand for the book. "We'll take it."

Serena reluctantly gave the sketch pad over.

"If you must know, Henry and I were basically living together before he was kidnapped," Elizabeth explained.

"Kidnapped? That's a very heavy accusation," Gaston remarked.

Oliver backed up his friends. "It's the truth."

"I gave her the key to my old studio," Henry added. Elizabeth nodded as she clung to him, afraid that if she stopped touching him, Henry would somehow disappear.

"This is Henry, me, and Oliver at Henry's last showing." She offered a photograph to Dr. Keller. It showed two couples standing beside a painting with their arms around each other; Elizabeth with Henry, who was sans beard, and Oliver and a blonde woman who the doctor hadn't met.

"What about your husband?" Gaston inquired.

"These are from pulling Arthur off of my son." Elizabeth pulled up her sleeves so the doctors could see the scars. "The psycho took after my baby with a box cutter!"

Henry's brow shot up and his eyes grew big. "I'm going to freaking kill him," he vowed.

"You did not just say that," Gaston interjected. "You know now that if something happens to him, I have to report it. It's the law."

"If you had seen what happened to the boy, I think you'd be inclined to look the other way," Oliver said. "Richard spent a week in the hospital."

"Arthur is the one that should be in here, not Henry," Elizabeth asserted.

"I'll get working on his discharge papers," Dr. Keller said.

"Are you serious?" Gaston interjected.

"He could sue both you and Talbot for malpractice," Dr. Keller responded. "This is a liability issue for the hospital. His identity has been established and validates what he's been saying. I am releasing him."

"Thank you," Henry replied.

"How long will the discharge process take?" Elizabeth inquired. "I'd like to reunite Henry with his son as soon as possible."

"Maybe twenty minutes," Dr. Keller answered.

"I can still take this to the board," Gaston reminded him.

"That would be an unwise decision, *Dr.* Bell," Elizabeth said with enough sarcasm in her tone to let him know what a joke she found that title to be.

"I can have fifteen reporters down here with one phone call," Oliver threatened. "It's not worth it to dig in your heels."

"Just let them go," Dr. Keller instructed. This could turn into a PR nightmare.

She grabbed Henry by the hand. "We're leaving now." Elizabeth guided him toward the door. Oliver scooped up the documents Elizabeth had brought with her.

"You can't just take a patient from the facility," Serena protested.

"Watch me!" Elizabeth threw over her shoulder. In a matter of moments, she and Henry were out the door. Oliver flanked them. He glared at anyone who even looked as though they were thinking of stopping the trio.

They hustled outside. Elizabeth hurried Henry into her car while Oliver got in his.

They didn't get too far. They were only on the road a matter of minutes before everything got to be too much for Elizabeth. She had to pull over and park in a parking lot. Elizabeth gripped the steering wheel tightly. Closing her eyes, she laid her face down on her arms.

"Are you all right?" Henry inquired.

Elizabeth sniffled and turned her head to look at him. "Yeah." She reached out and cupped his cheek. "I'm sorry I didn't find you sooner."

"I know you were trying." Henry reached out and patted her knee. When he realized he was touching her, he stopped and pulled his hand back abruptly. "I'm sorry," he muttered.

"No, it's OK. I don't mind," Elizabeth assured him. She

retrieved a three-by-five out of her purse. "This was taken a week ago." Elizabeth handed it to Henry.

Speechless, he scanned the photograph.

"Richard is adorable, isn't he?" Elizabeth said.

Henry nodded, his eyes still glued to his little doppelganger with a mop of blond hair and the biggest blue eyes. Henry's eyes shone with unshed tears.

"He's grown so big." Henry cleared his throat.

"You missed a lot," Elizabeth acknowledged sadly. "He's going to need both of us to help him get over what Arthur put him through," Elizabeth said.

"Where is Richard?" Henry asked.

"I had just dropped him off with his tutor when Oliver called," Elizabeth informed him.

"He's not even five yet, and he has a tutor?" he questioned.

"She's a glorified speech therapist really," she replied.

"What's wrong with his speech?" Henry frowned.

"Nothing he won't grow out of. Richard has a little trouble with Hs and he developed a fearful stutter. It only comes out with certain people," Elizabeth said.

Henry set his jaw. He could just bet he knew who the certain person was.

"I thought about picking him up, but I didn't know what I'd find when I got there," Elizabeth admitted.

"I'm glad actually. I wouldn't want him to see me like that," Henry said. He looked down at the patient scrubs that he was still wearing. He sighed. "Like this."

Elizabeth nodded. "Not the best first memory for him to have of you."

Oliver came up to the driver's side door. He knocked on the window. Elizabeth rolled it down. Oliver looked over his friends. "Is everything OK?" he asked.

Both Elizabeth and Henry tipped their heads. "I just needed a moment," she answered.

"Is there any way I could get cleaned up?" Henry requested. "I don't want to scare Richard."

"Don't worry," Oliver said. "We'll take care of you."

Chapter Three

H enry stepped out of the shower and grabbed the waiting towel. He wiped the water off his newly clean face. Henry dried his hair briskly. He rubbed the condensation off the mirror. The man revealed was someone he hadn't seen in a long time.

He found the clothes Oliver had brought him and got dressed. Henry hung up his towel on a drying hook as he exited. He made his way through Oliver and Miranda's bedroom and down the stairs to find Elizabeth and Oliver waiting for him in the living room.

The full effect of the haircut and new outfit was stunning. The powder-blue shirt made Henry's blue eyes pop. There was the man who had stolen her heart.

"Wow," Elizabeth remarked breathlessly. Her hazel eyes roamed over him.

A smile tugged at the corner of Henry's mouth. He made a mental note to never grow out his hair or another beard again.

"Feel better?" Oliver asked.

"I'm human again," Henry marveled.

Oliver smiled. "A fresh shave and haircut can work wonders."

"The shower too. Thanks for letting me get that smell off and, well, everything," Henry replied.

"Don't mention it. What are friends for?" Oliver said.

Henry smiled softly. "You're a rare breed of friend."

"And you are stuck with me." Oliver smirked. "Lucky you."

"Where to next?" Henry inquired.

"Jessica took Richard to the park," Elizabeth said.

"The park then," Henry replied.

Elizabeth offered him her hand. "Let's go get our son." He looked between her eyes and her hand. Henry tentatively accepted her hand.

"I'll follow you guys," Oliver offered.

Henry was quiet on the ride to the park. Elizabeth remained silent to give him space to think. She unbuckled and turned to look at him. "Want to talk it out before you see him?" Elizabeth inquired.

"What is Richard going to think of me?" Henry hung his head.

Elizabeth caressed the back of Henry's hand. "He's going to feel how much you love him."

"Have you been able to talk to him about me?" Henry inquired.

"Not as much as I would have liked to," she answered. Elizabeth licked her lips. She fumbled with putting her keys in her purse. "He doesn't know," Elizabeth added.

"He thinks Arthur is his dad?" he questioned.

"I didn't give him that impression. Dad and Arthur,

they …" She trailed off and then sighed.

Henry frowned. "Bulldozed their wishes over yours as usual."

"The title *daddy* or *father* doesn't have very good connotations for Richard," Elizabeth admitted.

"I can imagine why." He dipped his head.

"I'm sorry, Henry," she replied.

"None of this is your fault," Henry said.

"We wouldn't be in this spot if I hadn't agreed to this mock marriage." Elizabeth hung her head.

"We both know why you did." He looked out the window. For a moment neither of them spoke.

She broke the silence. "I don't think telling Richard is something we can just jump into."

"After all this time, I need to prove myself to him," Henry agreed.

Elizabeth cupped his cheeks in her hands. Hope radiated from her. "I know it's not going to take long. He is going to fall in love with you just like his mama," she insisted. Elizabeth could have sworn she saw Henry wince. He pushed through to a smile as if to hide the first expression.

They got out of the car. Oliver joined them as they left the parking lot and entered a large area in the park set aside for a playground.

"Mama!" Richard waved at her from the top of a slide. Elizabeth walked over to the slide. She stood at the bottom and held up her arms to catch him.

"Come on, angel." Elizabeth motioned for him to come down. Richard slid down and into his mother's hands. He squealed as she lifted him into the air. Henry's heart swelled within his chest until he felt it about to burst at the sight.

The tutor gathered her things. "Thanks, Jessica." Elizabeth waved.

The other woman waved back as she left. "See you later."

Elizabeth headed for a nearby bench as the guys followed. She sat down with Richard on her lap. Elizabeth craned down to lock eyes with her son. "Honey, there is someone here I want you to meet." She patted the bench beside them. Henry took that as a signal to sit. "This is my friend Henry. Can you say hello, angel?" Elizabeth instructed.

The child echoed a soft, bashful, "'Ello." He nuzzled into his mother.

"Hi." Henry blinked. "Wow, I bet you don't remember me. You were a tiny baby the last time I saw you."

Richard looked to Elizabeth. "Mommy has known him for a long time," she confirmed. "Remember I showed you his picture?"

Richard's brow furrowed. "T'e picture on your nightstand?" Henry tried to hide a smirk.

"Henry is going to be staying with us," Elizabeth informed her son. Richard visibly tensed.

"Is that OK with you?" Henry asked.

"If not, Henry can come stay with me." Oliver walked up behind Henry.

"Uncle Ollie!" Richard jumped up and ran to hug Oliver.

"Hey, Ricky." Oliver mussed the little moppet's blond hair.

Richard pulled away and began to look around.

"Oh, I'm sorry, bud. Ophelia's not here," Oliver explained. "She and Orlando are visiting with their Grams."

Richard sagged. "Oh."

"You know, Henry's my friend too." Oliver squeezed

Henry's shoulders. Henry bit the inside of his cheek and nodded. He knew what Oliver was doing, but that didn't make it any easier. Henry had to be vouched for with his own kid, and it burned.

He spotted a certain piece of play equipment out of the corner of his eye. "Will you push me on the swing?" Richard requested.

"I can't stay too much longer, but tell you what: Henry likes swings and I bet he would love to push you." Oliver winked.

"Can I?" Henry requested.

Richard paused for a moment, a thoughtful look in his eyes. Henry must be safe if Uncle Ollie liked him, he decided. Uncle Ollie didn't like people who'd hurt Mama. "If Mama comes too," Richard agreed.

"Of course I will," Elizabeth said.

Henry stood and held out his hand to help Elizabeth up. Richard frowned slightly. He wasn't sure what to think of that. Elizabeth kept hold of Henry's hand after she was on her feet, so Richard went around and grabbed her other hand. They set off together while Oliver hung back. He couldn't help smiling, watching his friend. Henry was back where he belonged. The trio needed some family time. He'd check in later to see how it went. Henry looked back and waved at his friend. Oliver waved back and then made his way back to his car.

Richard chose the closest swing. He settled down into the swing's seat and took hold of the chains.

"That's a big swing, isn't it?" Henry remarked. It made Richard look a bit small, which he was for his age. "Are you ready?" Henry asked.

Richard nodded. "Yes."

"Hold on tight," Henry directed. Richard tightened his grip. Henry pulled the swing back and let it go, starting slowly and gently at first.

"Move your legs, baby," Elizabeth coaxed.

Richard began to pump his legs at her urging. Henry began to push a little faster. Richard began to go higher and higher.

"T'ank you, Ri," Richard skipped to the last part of the name because of his problems with Hs.

Henry scanned the playground for something else he and Richard could play on together. "Those monkey bars look fun." Henry motioned with his head toward the metal structure. "Want to try them?"

"I'm too small." Richard shook his head. "I fall."

"You won't fall if we work together," Henry offered.

"Henry won't let you fall," Elizabeth encouraged.

Once he got to the top rung, Henry took hold of Richard by the waist.

"Don't let go," Richard entreated.

"I won't let go," Henry promised.

Richard reached for the first bar and then the next and the next. Henry acted as a support, letting Richard do the work of keeping himself up but taking just enough strain off his little arms.

"Come on! You can do it, angel!" Elizabeth cheered from the opposite side.

"You got it, little prince," Henry encouraged. One bar at a time, Richard and Henry kept moving. Richard cheered when he reached the last bar.

"I did it!" Richard beamed. Henry carried him around to his mother.

Elizabeth clapped. "I'm so proud of you." She took Richard's face in her hands and gave him an Eskimo kiss. Henry set him on his feet.

"Who wants a milkshake?" Elizabeth asked.

"*Me!*" Richard called and Henry made sure to answer at the same time.

"What kind do you want, angel?" Elizabeth inquired.

"Can I have strawburry?" Richard asked.

"Whatever kind you want is fine." She straightened the collar of Richard's polo shirt.

"Strawberry is my favorite." Henry smiled. "It's been a long time since I had a milkshake."

"We are going to have to fix that aren't we, angel?" Elizabeth bopped Richard's nose. The little boy giggled.

Henry smirked. "You're going with your usual, I presume."

She snickered. "You can't go wrong with chocolate."

———

The trio headed over to the elevators of the high-rise where Elizabeth and Richard now lived. One emptied as they approached, so they entered.

Elizabeth lifted her son in her arms. "You know our button," she encouraged. Richard pushed the button for the penthouse floor. It lit up. Once on his feet, Richard dutifully returned to his spot by his mother as the doors closed. The whole way up, the boy kept tabs on Henry. He still wasn't sold on this newcomer yet. They got up to the floor without too many stops. He set down the shopping bag of new clothes that

Oliver had bought him.

"This is a nice place," Henry remarked.

"We've been here about six months now," Elizabeth said.

"This is more your style than the mansion," he noted.

"I'm thinking we should order in tonight," she remarked.

"All right," Henry said.

"How does pizza sound?" Elizabeth suggested.

"Yummy!" Richard cheered.

"I'll call in the pizza. Any special requests?" Elizabeth asked.

"I'm more than grateful just to be here. Get whatever you and Ricky like," Henry answered.

"Large cheese and a salad it is," she said before heading for the phone.

Richard put his shoes away in the closet. Henry stayed behind with him, taking off his own shoes, while Elizabeth crossed the room to a hutch after placing the order.

She opened a drawer in the hutch and pulled out a credit card–sized envelope. Elizabeth tugged the top flap free. Squeezing it open, she worked out a metal key.

Henry straightened from placing his shoes in the closet and closed the door behind him and Richard.

Elizabeth approached Henry and lifted his hand. She placed the key in Henry's palm and closed his fingers around it. "You might need this."

"Thanks," Henry said. "I need to get a key chain or something."

"Hey, angel, why don't we show Henry your room while we are waiting on dinner?" Elizabeth suggested.

"OK." Richard bounded up the stairs.

Henry and Elizabeth followed at a more reasonable pace.

The only art supplies he noticed were a stack of coloring books and a couple boxes of crayons. They all looked brand new and the crayons remained unopened. To be fair everything looked brand new. There was no children's art on the walls, though they were painted a soft sky-blue; a very calming color.

A framed picture of Elizabeth and Richard was on the nightstand.

"That's a big bed for such a small boy," Henry remarked. It had to be queen sized. There were steps on one side for Richard to easily get in and out.

Richard shrugged. "Mommy sleeps in it with me sometimes."

"Who is that?" Henry pointed to a yellow teddy bear that sat next to Richard's pillow.

"Lucy." Richard snatched the bear off his bed. He proudly presented Lucy to Henry.

"What a pretty bear." Henry reached out and shook the bear's paw. "It's nice to meet you, Lucy."

Richard giggled.

"Your fur is very soft," Henry added.

"I like soft t'ings." Richard hugged his bear.

The doorbell rang. "That must be our food," Elizabeth said.

She handed Henry thirty bucks. "Tell the delivery guy to keep the change."

Elizabeth and Richard went to set the table while Henry answered the door and paid the guy for the food.

He met them at the table. "What would you like to drink?" Elizabeth asked.

"Water would be great," Henry answered. She exited. He

began to divvy out the food.

Richard got into his chair. "I bet you like pizza," Henry said.

"I like it a lot," Richard replied.

"Do you get pizza every night?" Henry grinned.

Richard shook his head. "We only get pizza when Mama's 'appy."

Elizabeth returned, beaming as she set down the drinks. "I hope I got you enough ice," she said.

"Filled to the brim, just how I like it." Henry winked.

The two parents sat down. Elizabeth folded her hands and bowed her head as did Richard. Henry followed suit. "Please, bless this food we are about to eat. Thank you for your wonderful mercies. We especially thank you for bringing Henry back. We are eternally grateful to have him with us. Amen," she prayed.

Henry took his first bite. "Mmm, this is good pizza," he remarked.

"Glad you like it," Elizabeth replied. "What do you think, angel?" Richard had his mouth full so he gave her a thumbs-up sign.

Soon the pizza box sat emptied on the dining room table. All that was left of the salad was remnants on their plates.

"May I go play, Mama?" Richard requested.

"All right with me. Henry and I will be up after we take care of the dishes. We won't be long," she directed.

Henry put the pizza box and salad container in the trash while Elizabeth rinsed their plates and put them in the dishwasher.

For a second time, Elizabeth and Henry climbed the stairs together. They found Richard on his stomach playing with a pair of cars. "Time to get you into your PJs," Elizabeth said.

"Ok, Mama," Richard replied.

"Top drawer?" Henry motioned to the dresser.

Elizabeth nodded. Richard got his shirt stuck as he tried to take it off over his head. She tugged him free. Henry retrieved a matching set of pajamas. He turned around to give it to them. Henry froze the moment his eyes landed on his son's back. He set his jaw. His blood began to boil. The scars from the box cutter incident were much more pronounced than the ones on Elizabeth's arms.

She noted Henry's reaction, but she didn't say a word. Elizabeth accepted the PJs from him with sympathetic eyes.

Richard switched pants and then slid his arms into the shirt. She buttoned the buttons for him. "Now go pick a story." Elizabeth flicked her head toward the bookcase.

She pushed up off her knees and went to Henry. Elizabeth wrapped her arm around Henry's waist. "I should have been there to protect him," Henry said in a low, shame-filled tone. She laid her head on Henry's shoulder.

Richard chose a collection of fairy tales. He turned around to give the book to his mom. Seeing their closeness, Richard stopped short. Henry swallowed. "That the one you want?" He tried to keep his voice steady.

Richard nodded, holding the book out. Henry took it with a smile.

Elizabeth sat on a beanbag. Richard grabbed Lucy and jumped into Elizabeth's lap. Henry settled in next to the beanbag and opened the book.

"Once upon a time," Henry began to read. Richard listened with rapt attention to every word. When the first story was finished, Henry kept on reading the next story and then the next. He got no complaints from Richard.

"And they all lived happily ever after," Henry finished. Richard yawned.

"I think story time is over. You need some sleep," Elizabeth announced.

"Can I have a hug?" Henry requested. Richard glanced at Elizabeth momentarily hesitating. She nodded her approval. Richard walked toward Henry with raised arms. Henry knelt on the ground so Richard would have better access. He wrapped his arms around his son gingerly. His lips pressed together to fight tears welling inside. Elizabeth wiped her eyes with her hand.

Richard pulled away first. "Night, Ri." He batted his eyelashes.

"Sweet dreams, little prince." Henry smiled.

Elizabeth turned down the comforter. Richard climbed into his bed.

Richard kissed her cheek. "Good night, Mama."

"Goodnight, angel. See you in the morning." Elizabeth kissed his forehead. Richard snuggled down into his pillow. She pulled the covers up past his shoulders.

Henry picked up the teddy bear from the beanbag. "Don't forget Lucy." He held her out to Richard.

Richard reached out for the plushy. He brought the bear under the covers and squeezed Lucy tight. Elizabeth switched off the light.

She and Henry went down to the living room so they could talk and let Richard sleep.

Elizabeth plopped down on the couch. "Five stories?" She raised an eyebrow.

"I've got a lot of bedtimes to make up for." He joined her

sitting.

"I always knew you'd be an excellent dad," Elizabeth replied.

"He's scared of me," Henry noted.

"I wouldn't say scared. He's leery of men in general," she said. "Oliver is really the only guy Richard fully trusts."

"I'm glad he stepped in," he replied.

"It's nothing you did," Elizabeth encouraged.

"How bad?" Henry cleared his throat. "How bad did things get?"

"I got used to being knocked around. Arthur started on Richard once he could walk and things escalated from there," she answered.

"To Arthur taking a box cutter to a four-year-old." He fought the urge to clench his fists.

"That was how I got Dad to let us move out," Elizabeth replied. "It took Richard nearly dying for him to see he wasn't safe around Arthur."

Henry bit the inside of his cheek. "Duncan is either unbelievably stubborn or —"

"Completely dense?" she finished for him.

"Sorry. I shouldn't talk about your father like that." He rubbed the back of his neck.

"I inherited my stubbornness from him." Elizabeth shrugged one shoulder. She glanced at her watch. "It's getting late," she remarked. "We should probably get some sleep."

"I guess the couch is my friend tonight," Henry said.

"Or you could sleep in my room. There is a spare bedroom if you'd be more comfortable with that," Elizabeth offered.

"The spare room might be wise," Henry agreed.

Her heart sank. "All right. I need to go get you a clean set of sheets." She stood. "I don't even think I've made that bed."

Elizabeth headed for the linen closet, but before she got out of reach, Henry reached out and touched her arm. The contact stopped her in her tracks. He didn't try to grab her.

Henry waited for Elizabeth to look at him. "For now, I think it's best if we take things slow." He got to his feet. "Rebuild, you know."

"Right." Her shoulders fell.

"I don't want to hurt you." Henry tucked a stray strand of her hair behind her ear.

She let herself breathe and listened to him.

"I have had people messing with my mind for five years," he continued. "More than one doctor told me our relationship was all in my head."

"You know it was real, all of it." Elizabeth rested her hands on his chest.

"The logical side of me does, and Richard, he's the ultimate proof," Henry admitted. "But being told day in and day out that I'm crazy has its effects."

She locked eyes with him. "You're still my Henry."

He sighed. "Let's see if you like the version that came back from the asylum."

Chapter Four

A whimper woke Henry from his sleep. He blinked his eyes open. In the dark it was hard to remember where he was. The surroundings were new. The whimpering continued. Henry threw off his blankets. He followed the sounds up to Elizabeth's room.

He found Elizabeth restlessly tossing from side to side. "No!" she sobbed.

"Elizabeth?" Henry said in a voice just above a whisper.

Elizabeth continued to thrash. "Stop!"

Henry reached out and laid a tentative hand on her shoulder. He repeated her name a little louder.

"Let me go!" She woke with a start. Elizabeth forcefully grabbed hold of Henry's wrist, holding it away from her as she shot up.

"Hey, hey, hey …" Henry put a finger to his lips.

It took a moment for her to register who was in the room with her. She pressed their joined hands to her chest. Elizabeth tried to even out her breathing.

"Are you OK?" Henry asked. His concerned eyes roamed

over her.

"Did I wake him?" Elizabeth questioned. She leaned over to look toward Richard's habitually open door. There was no light or movement.

"I think he is still fast asleep," he assured her quietly.

"Good." Elizabeth swallowed. Their doors were left open so Elizabeth could hear his cries and get to him quickly in the case of a nightmare—not for him to hear hers.

She closed her eyes in a futile effort to calm herself. An image of an angered Arthur flashed before her. Suddenly Elizabeth felt her body being pressed down. "Stop your whining!" a voice only she could hear commanded. Her eyes popped open wide.

"It's just a memory," she repeated mentally.

"Your heart is pounding," Henry remarked. The moonlight lit his face. His eyes were soft; his smile comforting. Henry stroked her cheek with his free hand. "What's wrong?" he inquired.

Elizabeth couldn't find her voice. She relished his touch. Elizabeth pressed her lips to the pad of his hand. She looked up at him only moving her eyes. They communicated what Elizabeth couldn't.

Henry's smile faltered just a little. "Is there anything I can do for you?"

"Can you hold me until I fall back asleep?" Elizabeth requested.

"All right," Henry agreed. She pulled back the covers and moved over to give him space. He slid into the spot.

Elizabeth cuddled into him. Her head and a hand came to rest on his chest. Henry wrapped an arm around her.

"I'm here now," he consoled. "You can sleep. Everything

is going to be OK."

She sighed, almost afraid to believe the words, but maybe, just maybe, he was right.

⸻

Richard squeezed his eyes into narrow slits to fight against the bright light of the dawn. He shuffled his feet on the hallway carpet. It wasn't too far to his mother's room. Richard stopped at the side of his mother's bed. Someone was in his spot.

Feeling little eyes on him, Henry woke up, inhaling sharply. "Hey, little prince," Henry greeted groggily. Henry's hand came to rest on Richard's shoulder. The soft feel of Richard's jersey T-shirt reminded Henry that Henry was, thankfully, wearing pajamas.

Elizabeth popped her head up. "What's up, baby?" She licked her dry lips.

"You OK?" Richard asked.

"I was having bad dreams. Henry stayed with me to make me feel safe," she explained. Richard often climbed into his mother's bed, or she stayed with him in his because of nightmares so the explanation was easy for him to understand.

"You want to climb in?" she asked.

Richard nodded.

"C'mere." Henry lifted the boy into the bed. Richard cuddled in between his parents. In a matter of moments, he drifted dangerously close to sleep again. Henry's eyelids grew heavy once more. They threatened to shut on him.

"You two are peas in a pod!" Elizabeth chuckled. She kissed the crown of Richard's head and then Henry's brow.

"Mornings are overrated," Henry mumbled.

Elizabeth looked at the clock on the nightstand and read 6:00 a.m. It was still just a little early. They could sleep for another hour or two. She laid her head back down on the pillow. Her face and eyes glowed at seeing her son and the man she loved resting with serene faces. This view right in front of her? Oh, it was heaven.

After an hour of watching them, Elizabeth decided to leave her guys to sleep. She came down the stairs to start breakfast so it would be ready when they came down.

Retrieving a mixing bowl and mixer beaters, she set them on the counter. On her way up, she saw Henry and gasped.

"Good morning," he greeted. She squatted down and opened a lower cupboard.

"Hi." Elizabeth blushed lightly. "I thought you were asleep."

"You know the quickest way to get me out of bed is to leave yourself," Henry quipped. He wouldn't lie. Holding Richard was the next best thing to holding her. But it still wasn't the same.

"I didn't mean to abandon you. I just thought you and Richard might be hungry when you woke up," she explained.

A loud growl escaped from Henry's stomach. "You'd be right." He patted his side. "Is there anything I can do to help?" Henry offered.

"Well, I am thinking pancakes with strawberries and bacon for breakfast," she said.

"Sounds good to me," he agreed. "Do you want me to start the oven for the bacon?" Henry remembered she'd bake hers.

Elizabeth nodded. "The rack and a cookie sheet are in the drawer under the oven."

Henry rounded the counter. Going to the stove, he turned the oven knob to the appropriate temperature and then got out the cookie sheet. She retrieved the whipping cream from the fridge.

They went about the kitchen, gathering utensils and breakfast ingredients. Their movements slowly formed a kind of dance around each other.

Elizabeth put the whipped cream into the refrigerator. Then she began measuring the ingredients for the pancake batter. Henry stopped what he was doing and leaned on the counter. He couldn't stop staring at Elizabeth.

"Penny for your thoughts?" the object of his affection proposed as she stirred.

"I was just remembering the first time you made me pancakes." Henry grinned.

"Please, let's not relive the hockey-puck incident." Elizabeth laughed.

"They weren't that burnt," he said and chuckled.

"I set off the smoke detector," she countered.

"I still ate them," Henry replied.

"Yeah, you did." She paused, gazing at him with big doe eyes.

Unable to help himself, he captured her lips with his. Pulling back a touch startled, Elizabeth was the one to break off the kiss. He couldn't quite read the look in her eyes. Henry cleared his throat. "Too soon?"

"No, no, no." Elizabeth shook her head. "It was just a happy surprise." She reached out and took his face in her hands. "I liked it." Elizabeth drew him into a second lingering kiss. After they parted she nuzzled his nose for good measure.

He sensed a hint of sadness in her. Were the kisses not

measuring up to the way they used to feel?

"I have taken some cooking classes so these pancakes should be much better," she said. Elizabeth got a frying pan heating. "Could you wash the strawberries?" she requested. "There are some fresh ones in the fridge."

Before she could pour the first pancake, a knock sounded on the door. Elizabeth turned off the burner and set the batter on the counter. Security wouldn't let just anyone up to this floor, so something had to be happening.

She opened the door and came face to face with the last person in the world she wanted to see. Her blood ran cold.

Elizabeth tried to slam the door in his face, but he grabbed the door jam and the door bounced back off his arm. "What kind of greeting is that for your husband?" Arthur chided.

Elizabeth steeled herself. She would never let him know just how much he made her stomach churn. "Leave now. Don't make me call security," Elizabeth commanded.

Henry stopped cleaning the strawberries in the sink and raced to Elizabeth's side.

Arthur ignored her protest and the other man's presence. He stepped inside. "Duncan is asking when you and Richard are coming home."

"How about when hell freezes over?" Henry growled.

They heard a door close upstairs. "There he is," Arthur remarked.

"And he'll stay there until you go." Elizabeth crossed her arms over her chest.

"I guess that's your way of saying I don't get to see Richie," Arthur said.

Henry's muscles flexed like a boxer readying himself for a fight. No way in hell that was happening.

"No, you do not," Elizabeth stated firmly.

Arthur shrugged. No skin off of his nose. "Duncan is becoming impatient. We had a deal," he continued.

"Richard was never part of the deal!" Henry thundered. "I never agreed to let you have any claim over my kid!"

"Watch the volume, Picasso," Arthur snapped. He glanced up the stairs.

"We are telling Richard I am his father sooner or later. Can't be soon enough for me," Henry asserted.

Arthur looked over to Elizabeth. "Is that right?"

"We can't keep Richard's real paternity from him forever," she replied.

"What about Duncan? Have you even thought about how he's going to react?" Arthur questioned.

"Considering how much Richard resembles Henry, I'm pretty sure Dad already knows," Elizabeth asserted.

"Then why hasn't he said anything?" Arthur challenged.

"You don't care if Richard finds out that he's my son." Henry sneered. "You care that someone just might tell Duncan. It's going to come out."

"You might want to think of the cost to Richard should Duncan find out," Arthur advised.

"He's still Dad's flesh and blood," Elizabeth asserted. "Which is more than you can say."

Arthur's nostrils flared. He saw red. Arthur charged toward Elizabeth. Henry stepped into his path. "Don't even think about it." Henry straightened to his full height.

"Or what, pretty boy?" Arthur snapped.

"I want a divorce," Elizabeth insisted.

"You know Duncan is never going to allow that," Arthur replied.

"Guess we'll see," Henry countered.

"Do you really want to be the reason for Elizabeth's fall from grace?" Arthur questioned.

"Get the hell out!" Henry commanded.

"That was low even for you, Arthur," Elizabeth reprimanded.

"You need to leave," Henry insisted. He shoved Arthur out of the penthouse. The door closed behind them.

Elizabeth rushed to the phone. She dialed a number she knew her father would pick up. He answered with his name. "What the hell was Arthur doing coming here!" Elizabeth demanded. "Do not tell me to calm down!"

Henry returned after seeing Arthur to the elevators as she continued arguing over the phone. "It is not OK for him to show up at the penthouse," Elizabeth said. "You need to keep him away like you promised!" Elizabeth hung up and wiped her eyes with the back of her hands.

"Elizabeth?" Henry placed a hand on her shoulders.

She stood. "Richard must be starving."

Henry followed Elizabeth as she went to get her keys. "Richard knows to lock the door," she explained. Elizabeth chose a key as they headed for the stairs.

Elizabeth knocked on Richard's door. "It's Mama and Henry. I'm going to unlock the door, and we're coming in, OK?" She only got a muffled answer. Elizabeth turned the key and opened the door.

"Ricky?" Henry called. They boy was nowhere to be seen, and Lucy was missing too.

"Honey, where are you?" Elizabeth beckoned.

"Mama?" Richard sniffled.

Elizabeth went over to the end of the bed. She got on her

knees and lifted the bed skirt. Elizabeth craned down to look under the frame. Two bright blue eyes peeked out at her.

"Come here." Elizabeth motioned him forward.

Richard crawled out, holding onto Lucy. He jumped up and wrapped his arms around his mother's neck, the teddy bear hitting her in the back. She could feel Richard trembling. Elizabeth stroked his hair. "It's OK. Arthur is gone, angel. He's gone," she assured her son.

Henry took tentative steps toward them. He reached out to rub Richard's shoulder. He thought better of it and retracted his hand.

"I'm sorry," Richard said.

"There's nothing to be sorry for. You did everything right," Henry insisted.

Elizabeth stood. She caught Henry's eyes. "Can you go ahead and feed Richard?" Elizabeth requested.

"Sure, but ..." Henry agreed.

She made sure Richard was looking at her before addressing him. "Angel, go down with Henry, and he'll get you breakfast."

"What about you?" Henry asked.

"I need a shower." She spun around and raced to her room.

Henry took Richard by the hand. "Let's go eat."

"Is Mama going to have breakfast?" Richard asked.

"I hope so, little prince. We'll make some extra pancakes for her." Henry glanced at Elizabeth's door as they passed it. "Wanna watch me cook the pancakes?" Henry asked.

"Yeah," Richard answered.

They got a step stool out. Richard stood on it and saw Henry manning the frying pan.

"The stove and pan are going to be hot," Henry cautioned. He turned on the burner. After a few regular circles, Henry tilted his head. He decided to surprise Richard with some shaped ones.

"An R!" Richard covered his mouth and giggled.

Henry divvied up pancakes onto the plates. Richard got off the step stool.

"Do you want whipped cream on your pancake?" Henry asked as he got the bacon out of the oven and set it on hot mats.

Richard nodded. Henry went to the refrigerator and brought out the already made cream. He put dollops on top of his and Richard's pancakes. "Ready to eat?" Henry picked up his and Richard's plates.

"Aren't we going to wait for Mama?" Richard frowned.

"You should eat like your mom said to," Henry insisted.

"OK." Richard followed Henry to the table.

Henry set the plates down in the proper spots and then lifted Richard into his booster seat.

"Did I do something bad?" Richard questioned.

"What? No." Henry shook his head. "Why would you think that?"

"Daddy came 'ere." Richard poked at his pancake. "'E's not supposed to. Granddad said so."

Henry set down his fork. He turned to Richard and leaned down with his elbows on his legs. "Arthur coming here had nothing to do with you. He's not happy I'm here," Henry admitted.

Curious, Richard tilted his head.

"He and I don't like each other very much," Henry explained.

Richard's shoulders dropped. His countenance fell.

"He's mean to your mom and you," Henry quickly added.

"I'll be good," Richard promised.

"You are a good boy." Henry smiled at him.

Richard's spirit seemed to perk up at the affirmation.

"Now what do you say we finish our food before it gets cold?" Henry took his fork back up.

When Elizabeth hadn't returned by the time Richard and he had finished eating, Henry took Richard into the living room and settled him with a few toys. Henry switched on the TV and found a cartoon that caught Richard's attention.

"Peter Pan." Richard smiled.

"Is this OK?" Henry inquired.

Richard nodded. "I like Peter Pan."

"I'll be back. I'm going to check on your mom," Henry said.

"OK," Richard replied. Toys could keep him occupied while the movie played.

Henry heard the hair dryer running as he approached Elizabeth's room. He sat in the armchair and waited. Elizabeth stepped out wrapped in a towel. She nearly jumped out of her skin. She clutched her clothes to her chest upon seeing Henry sitting there. He scanned her, trying to get a read on the situation. The towel couldn't hide much. Anywhere Elizabeth hadn't scrubbed raw was scaled red from the heat of the water.

"We saved some pancakes for you." Henry pushed himself to his feet.

"That's very sweet, but I'm not hungry," Elizabeth

declined. She went to the bed and began to spread out her chosen clothes for another look. "Where is Richard?" Elizabeth asked.

"He's watching Peter Pan," Henry answered.

Elizabeth tried to lighten the mood. "He's on a kick with that movie."

"I'm worried about you." Henry stepped closer to her.

She stiffened. "Henry … I can't right now."

"Something happened. It's why you pulled out of our kiss earlier," he insisted.

"The dream kind of threw me for a loop. I thought I was over the nightmares," she admitted.

"That was not a nightmare. It was a flashback," Henry asserted gently. "I heard enough in my time at Wonder Ridge to know."

"You were the one unfairly committed to that … institution." Elizabeth hung her head.

"Let's forget about that right now. This isn't just about me," Henry urged. "Can we sit?"

She obliged him. The two sat on the chest at the end of her bed. Elizabeth wrung her hands. "What happened?" Henry coaxed.

"Are you sure you want to know?" she returned.

"I'm not going anywhere," he assured her.

"You just might change your mind." Elizabeth raked her hand over her face.

"You know me better, Elizabeth. I can handle the truth." Henry grabbed hold of her hand.

"I tried to fight Arthur off, but he is stronger than me," she said, fingering the ends of the towel.

He straightened his spine and shoulders bracing for her

next words.

"Arthur raped me." Elizabeth paused there to let the information sink in.

Henry swallowed hard.

She could see tears welling up in his eyes. "It wasn't just one time. It happened on multiple occasions," Elizabeth added.

"Did you tell your dad?" Henry inquired. She nodded yes. "He didn't rein Arthur in?" Henry's brow furrowed.

"Arthur is my 'husband' and I 'need to learn my place,'" she answered.

Henry sneered. "We are *way* past the fifties." He bit his tongue and mentally counted to ten.

"Please, don't hide from me. Honesty, remember?" Elizabeth implored.

Henry nodded. "Are you OK?" he asked. The moment the words left his lips he knew it was a dumb question.

She patted his cheek in understanding. "Healing is a long process."

"Do you need anything? I mean, what can I do to help?" Henry scooted closer to her.

"You haven't changed as much as you think." Elizabeth chuckled softly.

"Have you talked with anyone about this? Other than Duncan?" he questioned. Henry couldn't bring himself to call the man her father.

"Oliver pulled us off of the estate a few times. He saw me completely messed up so he knows and Miranda does too; then Richard..." she began. Her heart began to beat a little bit faster.

"Richard what?" Henry queried.

RESTORATION

Elizabeth looked at the floor. "The last time, Arthur dangled Richard out of the third-story window and told me if I didn't stop resisting he'd drop him onto the driveway."

"Bastard," Henry muttered.

"That's not the worst part. He wouldn't let Richard out of the room until he was done," she added.

"So Richard saw?" Henry's eyes widened.

Elizabeth pressed her lips together and nodded. "I know he remembers," she whimpered. Elizabeth buried her face in Henry's chest.

Her tears soaked through his T-shirt to his skin. They burned him like acid. He held her silently until they subsided.

"I am sorry you went through all of that." Henry lifted her chin to bring them eye to eye. "I can't change what happened, but I am here now." Henry wiped the moisture off of her face.

"Mama?" Richard peeked his head in.

She cleared her throat so she could speak normally. "I'm right here, angel," Elizabeth said as she turned toward the door.

Henry motioned him over. He pulled Richard onto his lap.

"Did you have a good breakfast?" Elizabeth inquired.

"We saved you some pancakes," Richard reported.

"Henry told me." She put on a smile. Both Henry and Richard saw through it.

Richard took his mother's hand. "Mama, come eat," he pleaded. His blue eyes were now saucers. "Please?"

"Who can say no to that face?" Elizabeth kissed Richard's nose. "Just let me get dressed, OK?" She stood and gathered her clothes.

"Why don't we go and fix her up a plate?" Henry offered. Richard looked up at him and nodded. He hopped down and then waited for Henry to lead him downstairs.

Chapter Five

Miranda sat down in front of her vanity. She checked her freshly washed face in the mirror. Her nimble fingers retrieved a silver barrette from the vanity top. Miranda twisted her long blond locks into an updo and held them in place with the clip. Now that her hair was out of her face she began her makeup application.

Oliver came up behind her and placed his hands on her shoulders. "Hello, gorgeous." He kissed the top of her hair.

"I'm flattered, Mr. Tate, but I'm already spoken for." Miranda held up her left hand and flashed him her wedding ring.

"You could do so much better, Mrs. Tate." Oliver played along with a twinkle in his brown eyes. He pulled her body flush to his.

"Are the kids up yet?" Miranda spread out her makeup brushes.

"They are both still sound asleep." Oliver craned down and trailed kisses along her neck. Miranda moaned. She arched her neck for him.

"With our luck, they won't be for long," Miranda purred. He chuckled. The vibration against her skin sent a shiver down her spine. "Let's make it count." She scooted over. Oliver took the space offered on the bench. He smirked. Miranda wrapped her arms around his neck and drew him into a lip-lock. Oliver tilted his head to deepen the kiss.

The clock Miranda kept on her vanity began to beep. Oliver groaned. She reached out and hit the button to turn the alarm off. "Sorry. You know I have to get to work on time." Miranda licked her lips.

"Making any progress with this big client?" Oliver inquired.

"I wish. These negotiations are kicking my butt," Miranda muttered.

"You're gonna wipe the floor with 'em, babe," Oliver encouraged. He grabbed her face and began to kiss her once more.

"Not if I can't leave my house on time." She placed her hands on his chest to get some distance between them.

Oliver admired her with hooded eyes. "It's not my fault! You're irresistible and you know it," he crooned.

Miranda laughed. "Is that right?" He dived in, hoping for another kiss. Miranda turned her attention back to the makeup on the counter, denying him with the turn of her head. Undeterred, Oliver resumed nibbling on her neck.

"Go, go!" Miranda swatted Oliver away. "I need to finish putting my face on."

"Fine." Oliver pretended to pout. "I hear the natives stirring anyway."

Miranda selected a scarlet red lipstick from her collection. "I'll be down for breakfast." She waved as he exited the room.

RESTORATION

He stopped in on his youngest first. He found Ophelia sitting at her little play vanity, already wearing a dress-up princess dress. She hummed to herself as she brushed one of her favorite doll's hair.

"Good morning, Daddy," Ophelia greeted him.

"Good morning." Oliver squatted down for a hug.

"Is Mommy up?" she asked.

"Yeah," he answered.

"Is she going to brush my hair?" Ophelia inquired.

"Mommy's busy, but I can brush your hair," Oliver offered.

"OK!" she beamed. Ophelia handed him the brush off her vanity. He ran the soft bristles through silky, dark-chestnut locks the same shade as his own hair. "Will you braid it?" she requested.

"Sure thing, princess." Oliver nodded. He divided her hair into three sections and with well-practiced hands weaved them securely together.

"What do you want to do today?" Oliver inquired.

Ophelia thought for a moment. "Can we play with Ricky?" she asked.

"I can't promise it'll be today, but I'll call Aunt Liz and see when Ricky can play," Oliver said. He secured the bottom with one of her fuzzy hair ties. "How is that, baby girl? You hungry?"

"Uh-huh," she replied.

"Let's go find your brother and see what cook has made for us to eat." He stood. She took his hand as he led her out of the room.

Oliver got the kids settled at the kitchen table. Miranda breezed into the room and grabbed a travel mug of coffee their cook had waiting for her on the counter.

"Aren't you going to eat?" Oliver questioned.

"I am late," Miranda declined.

Oliver frowned. "Oh."

Miranda patted his check. She kissed him while he pouted. Miranda used her thumb to tenderly wipe the lipstick off his lips. "I'll see you guys after work." She kissed the crown of Orlando's head and then Ophelia's cheek.

"Go get 'em, tiger," he cheered after her retreating form. The cook came out and placed the plates in their places on the table.

Oliver was about to sit down when the phone began to ring. He blew out a breath. "Go ahead and eat," Oliver directed, "I'll be right back." He went to the kitchen phone and picked up the receiver. "Hello?" he answered.

"You do answer your phone."

"Hey, Alex," Oliver said.

"How is my highest-grossing client doing this morning?" the agent chirped.

"Great," Oliver replied. "Got another script for me?"

"I've got about ten sitting on my desk," Alex quipped.

Oliver chuckled. "You know I want to be free for the next pilot season, right?"

"Yeah, I know," Alex replied. "I'm not calling about a job."

"Oh." Oliver looked over at the kids.

"Someone called me looking for you and your friend," Alex said.

"Who?" his brow furrowed.

Alex consulted the paper with the name and number written down. "A Serena Wilson. Apparently, she's a nurse from Wonder Ridge."

"From that place we pulled Henry out of?" Oliver pursed his lips.

"She said something about needing to return some sketch pads. Should I set up a meet? I couldn't get her to mail them," Alex replied.

"Let me talk to Henry, and I'll get back with you," Oliver decided.

"OK, enjoy your day off. I'll be in the office. I'm glad you found your friend," Alex said as she signed off.

"Me too." Oliver hung up the phone and dialed Elizabeth's number.

Henry answered the call. "Hello."

"Damn, it's good to hear your voice." Oliver grinned.

"Yours too, brother." Henry leaned against the counter. "What's on your mind?"

"I actually have a few reasons for calling," Oliver answered.

"Shoot," Henry said.

"Ophelia is asking for a playdate with Richard," Oliver began with the most pleasant reason he'd called.

Henry smiled. "I'll have to check with Elizabeth about the schedule, but I am sure that can be arranged."

Elizabeth walked through carrying her plate to the table. "I've canceled Richard's session with Jessica for today, so if Oliver wants to meet this afternoon, that's fine," she offered.

"How does this afternoon sound?" Henry replied.

"Around one at your place?" Oliver suggested.

"That's fine," Henry replied.

"Good, I'll be bringing Orlando as well," Oliver informed him.

"They are both welcome." Henry smiled. "It'll be great to

see my godson again."

"He's not a toddler anymore," Oliver remarked.

"OK, what's next on your list?" Henry replied.

"It's not urgent. We'll talk about the rest when I get there," Oliver replied. "See you later."

Henry hung up the phone and went over to Richard, who was getting down from his chair.

"Guess who's coming over to play," Henry said.

"Fia and Orlando?" Richard asked hopefully. He'd overheard that it was Uncle Ollie the older man was on the phone with.

"That's exactly right." Henry grinned. "They'll be over this afternoon."

Richard ran toward the sound of the doorbell as fast as his little feet could carry him.

Henry opened the front door to Oliver. The two friends greeted each other with a warm hug. Ophelia peeked in from behind her dad.

"Fia!" Richard cheered.

"Ricky!" she returned. The two immediately ran off.

Oliver ushered his oldest child in.

"Hello, Uncle Henry," Orlando greeted.

"Is it really you, Orlando?" Henry questioned.

"Yep." Orlando bounced on the balls of his feet. His features were a perfect mix of his parents, but like his sister, he got his brown eyes and hair of the same color from his father.

"How old are you now?" Henry asked.

"Six," Orlando answered.

"Wow," Henry replied, "You've gotten so tall."

Orlando puffed up. "I'll be in first grade in the fall."

"Oh, my, you are growing up way too fast," Henry said.

"Tell me about it," Oliver quipped. "I'm starting to feel old." He patted his son on the back, letting him know he could go join his sister.

"Where's Liz?" Oliver questioned.

"The kitchen. She's talking with her agent." Henry motioned his head toward the stairs.

"How are things going?" Oliver asked.

"Other than Arthur making an appearance, we've made some progress," Henry replied.

"Son of a—" Oliver pressed his lips together. He looked over to where the kids were playing. They didn't need to hear him use the language he felt like using. "Have you and Liz had a chance to talk?" Oliver got back to the conversation.

"There have been a few tough conversations," Henry answered. "I think we're starting to get on the same page."

"Glad to hear it." Oliver nodded.

"Richard is amazing." Henry's eyes sparkled as he glanced toward his son.

"He's a lot like his dad," Oliver replied.

Ophelia walked over and tugged on her father's sleeve. She waited for him to make eye contact. Before she could speak, Oliver scooped up his daughter. Ophelia laughed as he rolled her up his arms and then he rested her on her back over his shoulder. Ophelia's braided hair dangled down underneath her. "This bundle of energy is my baby girl." Oliver grinned.

"It's nice to meet you, Ophelia." Henry angled his head so

he was upside down too, which got a giggle out of the girl.

"Say hi to Uncle Henry," Oliver directed.

"Hi." She waved at Henry from her upside-down position.

Oliver placed Ophelia on her feet. She quickly returned to her friend and brother, who were now building a tower with Legos.

"She's what? Six months younger than Richard?" Henry guessed.

"Yeah, we were just about to announce when you ..." He trailed off when Elizabeth swung the kitchen door open. She crossed the dining room and joined them.

"Hey," Elizabeth greeted the two men.

"What's shaking?" Oliver inquired.

Richard waved at his mother. She waved back. "Just getting reminded of my workload for the next two months," Elizabeth answered.

"See the tower, Mama?" Richard called.

"That's great, angel!" Elizabeth praised.

"Very sturdy," Henry remarked.

"Let's make it taller!" Orlando suggested.

"Yeah!" Ophelia concurred.

The children continued building until all the blocks were used up. They held their breath and stepped back.

"It's so cool," Orlando marveled.

"So cool," Richard echoed. It wobbled and then fell over. Richard looked over to Orlando and Ophelia to see their reaction.

"Richard's got a bunch of coloring books and crayons upstairs. Do you kids want to color?" Elizabeth suggested.

Orlando nodded profusely. The two younger kids soon followed suit.

RESTORATION

"They're on your desk, angel," Elizabeth reminded him.

Richard led Orlando and Ophelia up to retrieve the art supplies.

"What are we doing about Richard's birthday?" Henry inquired. "It's a big one."

Elizabeth watched the kids, making sure they were far enough upstairs that they couldn't hear her answer. "I've been planning on taking him and Oliver's family to Disneyland," she revealed.

"Really? Has he been before?" Henry asked.

Elizabeth shook her head. "I arranged a birthday party at one of the restaurants and few other special things," she added.

"That sounds great," Henry approved.

"The boy needs a little spoiling," Oliver agreed.

Elizabeth picked a stray hair off Henry's collar. "We just have to get you a ticket and we'll be all set," she said.

The children came down with the art supplies. They set up at the kitchen table. Henry grabbed the opportunity to grab his sketch pad. He stood back so he could get a good view of the children. This scene begged to be put down on paper.

After a few minutes, Elizabeth approached him, drink in hand. He looked up and saw the cup. "My mug." Henry grinned.

"And your coffee." Elizabeth winked at him. It was filled to the brim with ice water. Henry chuckled and took a sip.

"What are you working on?" Oliver made his presence known.

Henry flipped the sketch pad over to reveal an unfinished sketch of the three kids coloring a page together.

"When you get around to setting up your studio, I want a

painting of that," Oliver said. "You're still as talented as ever."

"Maybe with a pencil." Henry shrugged and then set his mug down on the counter. He brought the correct side back so he could continue drawing.

"I remember you could sling paint around with the best of them." Oliver drank some of his lemonade.

"I haven't painted since that commissioned piece right after Richard was born," Henry informed them.

"Seriously?" Oliver raised an eyebrow.

"They didn't let you paint?" Elizabeth frowned. Henry motioned his head in the negative.

"We've got to get your stuff out of storage," Oliver remarked. "Get a paintbrush in your hand and it'll all come back to you."

Henry changed the subject. "You said on the phone earlier that you had a few more things you wanted to talk about."

"What can you tell me about that nurse from Wonder Ridge?" Oliver inquired.

"Serena? Why would you want to know about her?" Henry frowned.

"She got my agent's number from when he set up the tour," Oliver explained. "She says she's got more of your sketch pads and wants to meet to hand them over."

"It's not worth it." Henry shook his head.

"Are you OK with losing your work?" Oliver frowned.

"I certainly don't want to see her, and you don't need the headaches she could cause with Miranda," Henry cautioned.

"Miranda has been a lot more secure since we had the kids," Oliver defended his wife.

"I wouldn't put it past Serena to try to insinuate her way into a movie star's life," Henry cautioned.

Oliver frowned. "What could she do? It's just a drop-off."

"Duncan probably had them removed by now, but I know she has received several reprimands for hitting on patients," Henry said.

"How do you know this?" Oliver asked.

"I heard a doctor or two lecture her. I saw at least one wife slap her," Henry reported.

"She make a pass at you?" Oliver raised an eyebrow.

Henry nodded. "A few." Elizabeth rubbed Henry's shoulder comfortingly. Her hand drifted down to rest on top of his. "She'd always get jealous when I drew Elizabeth," Henry added. He turned his hand over and squeezed hers.

"Sounds like she's the crazy one," Oliver remarked.

Henry took a sip from his coffee mug. "I believe so. She could go to a reporter and make a bigger deal of the meeting than what it is."

"Neither of you should go," Elizabeth said.

"So we're settled." Henry nodded and went back to his drawing.

"No, I still want the meet set up," she replied.

"But you said—" Henry began.

"I said the two of you shouldn't go. I'll do it," Elizabeth volunteered.

"I don't think that's such a smart play either," Henry protested.

"Why not?" she countered.

"There is a possibility Duncan is paying her to come forward and mess with your head," Henry argued.

"I've known girls like her all my life. I can handle one little vamp," Elizabeth asserted. "I want your art back."

"There are a couple of pieces I would love to have, but

honestly the rest are only scribbles in the grand scheme of things." Henry scrunched up his face.

"They're all special," Elizabeth protested.

"It would be worth it for special ones," Oliver proposed.

"I doubt they'd be in with the sketch pads. I tore the special ones out and hid them in my room," Henry revealed.

"I can see if she can get them," Oliver offered.

"They disappeared a few months ago." Henry's lip curled up slightly.

"Well, that sucks." Oliver frowned.

"Tough to complain now that I'm out of there," Henry replied.

Elizabeth smiled. "True."

"Now it's just waiting for the other shoe to drop," Henry said.

"Do you think Duncan is going to pull something?" Oliver questioned.

"He's always working something." Elizabeth rolled her eyes.

"I say it's time to rip off the Band-Aid." Henry frowned. He brought the sketch pad down. "Let's take Duncan out to dinner and set him straight."

"Easier said than done," Elizabeth said.

Henry brought the sketch pad down and let it rest against his leg. "I know Duncan won't want to hear it, and he will probably blow a gasket, but maybe once he cools down, it will help him let go."

"I'll make the call," Elizabeth agreed. "Hopefully by the time we can arrange something, we'll figure out the best way to tell him."

"I'm not sure how we can soften the fact that his

grandson's father is a man he hates," Henry replied.

"Hate might be a bit of an overstatement," Elizabeth interjected.

"After everything he did to break us up? Yeah, he hates me." Henry hung his head. After a beat he took up the sketch pad once again. He put the finishing touches on his drawing.

Orlando held up the book they were coloring in and showed off the page. "Look, Daddy!" Ophelia called.

"I like it—so very colorful," Oliver praised. The parents joined the kids at the table.

"Show them your work." Elizabeth nudged Henry. Henry complied, opening his book to the sketch of the kids. He showed it to them. They all cooed over it, but Henry focused on Richard.

"You drew that?" Richard questioned.

Henry nodded. "Do you like it?" Henry held his breath waiting for his son's response.

Richard nodded his head. "Do you have more?"

"That he does. Henry is an artist," Elizabeth answered.

Richard looked up at Henry with a bit of awe in his eyes. "Really?"

"Yeah, I even went to school for it," Henry answered.

"I wish I could draw," Richard said.

Henry smiled at him. "I could teach you a little, if you'd like."

Richard tipped his head bashfully.

"I think that's a wonderful idea," Elizabeth pronounced.

Chapter Six

Elizabeth squatted down to her son's level. "You know the drill, angel." Richard nodded. "We'll be back to pick you up after your session," she promised. Elizabeth kissed his cheek.

Richard kissed her cheek in return. "Bye, Mama." He waved to Henry and gave him a shy smile.

"Listen to Miss Jessica," Henry directed.

"Don't worry." Jessica smiled at the parents. "I'm sure Ricky will be an angel like he always is."

Reluctantly the pair backed out into the hallway and headed for the elevators.

"Is it always this hard to leave him?" Henry questioned.

"I'm afraid so," Elizabeth replied. "I have to keep reminding myself that it's only for a couple of hours."

He shrugged. "Good preparation for when he's ready for school."

"Dad's already talking about keeping him with tutors instead of school." She pressed the call button for the elevator.

Henry fingered his neck. "You don't sound too thrilled

with that idea."

"He needs to be with other children. You saw him with Ophelia and Orlando," Elizabeth pointed out.

"Ricky definitely perked up around them," Henry acknowledged. The elevator car showed up, and they stepped inside.

"But then again, I know not all children are going to be as nice to Richard as Oliver's kids. After all, there is Tommy," Elizabeth said.

"Tommy?" Henry's brow furrowed.

"Silvia and Arthur's son," she explained.

"She stuck around?" Henry blinked incredulously.

"And moved into the mansion," Elizabeth added.

"Duncan lets Arthur keep a second family under his roof?" he scoffed.

She laughed. "Long as Arthur doesn't publicly acknowledge them, Dad couldn't give a flying fig."

"Let me guess—like father like son?" He rolled his eyes.

"The poor kid has no chance of growing up any other way," she replied.

Elizabeth looped her arm through his. "Enough about them. Ready to get back into the world?" she asked.

"I was rather enjoying the time alone with you and Richard," Henry replied.

"That has been nice," Elizabeth agreed. *Slow*, but nice.

"Before we go get my clothes there is someone I need to see," he informed her.

Knowing who he was talking about, Elizabeth nodded. "I was wondering when you were going to ask about visiting her," she said. "Do you remember the way over?"

Henry nodded. "Streets might have changed in five

years."

The elevator beeped. The doors opened and the couple stepped out.

"Do you know of a place we can pick up some flowers?" he asked.

"A florist shouldn't be that hard to find. Can't have you showing up empty-handed, now can we?" Elizabeth said.

Henry got out of the car carrying his carefully selected bouquet of light-pink roses. Elizabeth rolled down the driver's side window. "I can wait in the car if you'd like some space," she offered.

"It's too hot," he objected. Henry crossed around the hood while Elizabeth rolled the window up. He opened the driver's-side door for her. She exited, long legs and feet first. He closed the door behind her.

They entered the cemetery through a rickety gate. The couple passed two dingy outbuildings. They walked down a narrow aisle between rows of graves until they came to the correct one. Henry crouched down and brushed off his mother's tombstone. It wasn't much of a stone—only a flat rectangle with her name etched in along with her birth and death dates; more cement than stone looking. The grass around it was overdue for a trim. He laid the roses down on her stone. "These are for you, Mom. I know they don't make up for the time I've been gone. I'm sorry."

Elizabeth hung back, trying not to eavesdrop. She was there if Henry needed her, but she also wanted to offer him some privacy to talk to his mom.

"I never meant to stay away so long," Henry continued. "It was kind of out of my control. I never forgot about you." He inhaled deeply and held the air in for several moments. Henry blew out the breath. "Richard has grown so much. His birthday is just a few weeks away now." He began to ramble on. "I missed the others." Henry hung his head. "I really wish you had lived to see your grandson," he continued. Henry wiped his eyes and glanced around. He shook his head. "I'm going to get you someplace better," Henry promised. "Once we get everything settled." He pressed a kiss to his fingertips and then transferred it to her stone.

Henry got up onto his feet and stood there silently staring for a moment. Elizabeth stepped forward touching his back. She snuggled into his shoulder. He rested his cheek against her hair. "Pink roses were her favorite," Henry remarked.

"I bet she would have made a wonderful grandmother." Elizabeth gazed up at him adoringly.

"Richard sure could use having her around right about now. Mom would be loving on him like there was no tomorrow." He sighed. They took a minute just to be silent. "Thank you," Henry said.

"I didn't do anything," Elizabeth protested.

"You understood I needed this," he countered.

"Ready to get you some more clothes?" she inquired.

Henry nodded and they turned around to follow their path out.

He glanced backward one last time as they left. "I'll be back soon, Mom."

"Don't you care that you haven't seen your son in six months?" Duncan crossed his arms over his chest. He directed a stern scowl toward his second in command.

Arthur stood tall under the chastising glare. The air in the small space grew dense from Duncan's pressure. "Of course, I do," he said, giving the answer Duncan wanted to hear.

"Act like it," Duncan said to straighten Arthur out. The elevator would be stopping soon. "I didn't call on Commissioner Virgil to drop the abuse investigation for you to twiddle your thumbs."

"As you have said," Arthur replied.

"I shouldn't have to repeat myself," Duncan retorted.

"I'm sorry, that came out wrong. It's just, I have been doing what you asked." Arthur raked a hand through his hair.

Duncan tilted his head. "You've been dragging your feet since we left the office."

"You know how Lizzie gets sometimes. This might make her dig her heels in," Arthur explained.

"She'll have no choice but to deal." Duncan rolled his eyes.

"She loves Ricky," Arthur acknowledged.

"It's time to man up, Arthur," Duncan continued. "I am sick of this hand holding."

Arthur frowned. "I know. I just thought Liz would come around by now."

"Since my daughter has no intention of initiating a reconciliation, it's up to you to make the first move," Duncan pronounced.

They exited the moment the doors opened. Down the hallway they turned. Duncan's stride matched one of a leader, confident and brisk. Arthur was at his heels.

"Tell me this is for the best," Arthur requested.

"It worked for me," Duncan said. He knocked on the door of the apartment where Elizabeth and Henry had left Richard not an hour ago.

Jessica left her pupil at the table and went to answer. She cracked open the door and stood in the gap.

Duncan tipped his head. "Ms. Wallace."

"Hello, Mr. Harper," Jessica greeted.

Duncan didn't wait to be invited in. He barged right in as if he owned the place. Arthur followed like his shadow.

Richard blanched completely white at the sight of Arthur. The boy wanted to scream, but he knew better. Screaming would make Daddy mad. Running would ensure a beating.

"Hello, Ricky." Duncan smiled as he spoke so his grandson would focus on him.

Richard knew his granddad expected a hug. He tentatively got out of his chair and slowly made his way toward his grandfather. He embraced Duncan, but not fully and as briefly as he could get away with. Richard let go before Duncan did. Richard kept his eyes on the floor. He sidestepped in Jessica's direction.

Duncan saw Richard shrink back, obviously scared.

"Ricky has been progressing nicely," the tutor praised as she stroked Richard's hair.

"Of course he is. He's a very bright boy," Duncan agreed. Richard batted his eyelashes bashfully at his grandfather.

Duncan scooped up Richard and headed for the exit. "Where are you taking him?" Jessica tried to reach for Richard but was blocked by Arthur.

As Duncan carried Richard out of the apartment Arthur got into Jessica's face. "Stay out of this. It isn't your fight," Arthur warned. Coolly he spun around and left, slamming the door behind him.

———

"When you said we were going to get me some clothes, I thought we were going to a storage place," Henry said.

"We will, but you need some new pieces too." Elizabeth turned off the engine.

"The clothes Oliver gave me are fine," he protested.

"Two shirts and a pair of jeans aren't going to cut it," Elizabeth countered.

"It could wait until we get my bank account sorted out; you shouldn't have to pay for everything." Henry frowned.

"After five years of false imprisonment, a new wardrobe is the least you are owed," she insisted. "Besides you need something dressier for dinner with Dad."

"Did he get back with you on a time for the restaurant he insisted on picking?" he inquired.

"He got reservations for Saturday at Mermount," Elizabeth relayed.

"Again?" Henry lifted one eyebrow.

She remembered. "Our first meal with him there didn't go well."

"I think the word *disaster* is appropriate," he agreed.

"This is our do-over," Elizabeth replied brightly.

"What can a kid eat there?" Henry asked.

"There is a chicken dish Richard's eaten before," she answered.

"How much has the menu changed?" he questioned.

"Quit stalling," Elizabeth said.

Henry huffed. She had to tug him inside by the hand. "Ms. Harper," an employee greeted.

"Thank you, Lee." Elizabeth tipped her head.

"Can I help you find something?" Lee inquired.

"We're just here to pick up some men's clothes," Elizabeth replied.

Lee guided them. "Right this way."

As they approached the men's department, Henry pointed out an obnoxious tie-dyed shirt on the mannequin on the front corner.

"Umm, no." Elizabeth shook her head. He chuckled.

"If you need any further assistance, just give me a holler." Lee excused herself.

They waded in among the different displays. Henry chose a soft T-shirt. "That blue is a great color on you." Elizabeth nodded her head in approval. She reached out and felt the material. Elizabeth grabbed a few more: a darker blue, then one in cherry, and another in mint green.

They came into the business section. A burgundy shirt caught his eye. He picked it up and checked the tag. Henry hissed at the price. He put the shirt back on the rack. "Do not look at the prices," Elizabeth directed, almost nonchalantly. She had to get him a suit and tie before he balked. Elizabeth picked up the shirt and a white one, adding it to the others.

Elizabeth spotted a section of gray suit pants that would go great with the blue dress shirt Oliver had already bought. She selected a pair in his old measurements, then a second one a size smaller in the waist just to be on the safe side. They found the matching jacket in the correct size. "OK, now you are going to have to try some of these clothes on," Elizabeth said. She took the T-shirts and sat in the waiting area.

"So have you been thinking about what Oliver mentioned yesterday?" she asked him through the door of the changing stall.

"What?" Henry's brow furrowed as fiddled with the buttons on the white shirt.

"Have you thought about a studio yet?" Elizabeth clarified.

Henry shook his head. "It's a little too early to make those kinds of decisions."

"I know the guest room in the penthouse isn't big enough or practical for a studio," Elizabeth said.

"With carpeted floor, it would be a mess," Henry agreed. He pulled on the smaller suit pants and tucked in the shirt before zipping the pants up and securing the button.

"We should probably rent you one," she continued.

"Maybe we should see how your dad retaliates before starting those kinds of plans," Henry suggested. "Things are probably going to get messy before they get better." Next came the jacket, which he slipped over his shoulders. Henry looked in the mirror and straightened the jacket. He crossed his fingers that this would do the trick. Henry opened the door and stepped out so she could see the outfit.

Elizabeth looked him up and down. Her eyes darkened. That man had no idea how hot he was. She motioned her finger in a circle. Henry spun around so she could get the full effect. "This fits you nicely." Elizabeth smiled.

"OK, I'll try on the burgundy shirt to see which you like better," Henry said.

"I'm getting both," Elizabeth insisted.

"Not happening, Elizabeth," he replied.

"Henry," she called.

Henry froze and then after a moment pivoted on his spot. "Yes."

Elizabeth stood and crossed to him. "I get this is a pride thing, but can you, please, let me enjoy buying you something nice? I like taking care of you."

"I should be taking care of you," he protested.

"You do. We take care of each other." She reached out and stroked his cheek with the back of her fingers.

His eyes fluttered. "All right."

"And I'll agree to table the studio discussion until after we meet with Dad," she conceded, "But we will get you back to painting."

"As big a part of me as painting is, you and Richard come first," he insisted.

"You do know that it isn't an either/or thing; you can paint and be with us," Elizabeth replied.

"I've missed so much." Henry took her hands. "I don't want to miss anymore because my nose is stuck in a canvas."

"Refusing to paint? A very unlike-Henry thing to do, but you give a very Henry-like explanation." She stroked the back of his knuckles with her thumb.

"Who says I'm refusing to paint?" he smirked. His lips faltered slightly, but he recovered.

Elizabeth frowned. "What are you holding back from me?"

Henry chewed on the inside of his cheek. "What if I can't paint?"

"OK, that makes zero sense." She frowned.

He voiced his worry. "What if I've lost it? My touch, ability, talent—whatever you call it."

Elizabeth raised an eyebrow. "Have you seen your own

sketches?"

"Pencils might as well be a world apart from paintbrushes," Henry protested.

"We need to get you in front of a canvas like yesterday," Elizabeth remarked.

"Maybe it's already too late," Henry countered with a slight shake of his head.

"Too late?" she questioned.

"I used to dream about mixing colors," he said, "Stretching canvas …"

"I remember you'd have a dream about a painting, wake up, and paint it." Elizabeth nodded.

His face fell. "I stopped having those dreams."

"Maybe now that you're free they'll come back. Give it a little time," she encouraged.

Henry changed back into his street clothes. After selecting a couple more items, the couple found Lee and paid for the purchase.

Outside they loaded the bags into the trunk of the car. They got inside and began to buckle. Their car phone started to ring. Elizabeth answered it.

Jessica sniffled. "Ms. Harper."

"Hi, Jessica," Elizabeth answered. "How is Richard?"

"His father came and picked him up," Jessica answered.

Elizabeth's stomach fell. She fought the urge to throw up. "I told you Arthur is not allowed to be alone with Richard," Elizabeth replied.

Henry turned to her. "What's going on?"

"Richard's grandfather was with him," Jessica replied. "I didn't see Mr. Corbin until after Mr. Harper came in."

"Did they say anything about where they were going?"

Elizabeth's heart pounded in her ears.

"It all happened so fast: Mr. Harper picked up Richard and they were gone before I could stop them. I am so sorry," Jessica replied.

"Thanks for calling." Elizabeth was shaking as she hung up.

"Is Richard OK?" Henry asked.

"We need to get to the estate now." She locked fearful eyes with him. "They took our baby."

Chapter Seven

H enry gripped the steering wheel so tightly his knuckles were white.

Elizabeth held the car phone up to her ear, tapping her fingers against it. "Come on, pick up," she demanded. The phone rang until it cut off. "Damn it!" Elizabeth slammed the receiver down hard.

Henry glanced over at her. Elizabeth's skin was similarly drained of color. She turned to stare out the window. Elizabeth hugged herself. The shaking had stopped or at least lessened. "He's not answering," she said.

"We're getting closer," Henry assured her.

"Now I'm wondering if we should have headed to the airport." Elizabeth's shoulders shagged.

"We're going to find him," he vowed. "I just got him back. I am not letting him get taken away from me again." She brought her hand up and pressed the back of her fingers to her mouth.

They were stopped at the gate by security. The guard on duty at the estate straightened to his full height as Henry rolled down his window. The guard looked past Henry and addressed the woman in the passenger seat. "Hello, Ms. Harper." He tipped his hat.

"Open the gate, Murphy," Elizabeth directed rather gruffly.

They'd barely parked the car when they ripped off their seatbelts. Not bothering to close their doors, Elizabeth and Henry stormed inside the mansion, meeting no resistance.

"Ricky!" Henry called.

With no response, she yelled for her father. They went deeper into the house.

Silvia heard the commotion and came downstairs. They came upon the staircase as she was hitting the bottom step. Silvia paled upon seeing Henry.

"Where is Richard?" Henry demanded.

"Um, I-I-I—" Silvia began to stutter.

"Please, where is my son?" Elizabeth pleaded.

"He's in the back playing with Tommy," Silvia blurted out.

Duncan entered at a lazy pace. "Liz—" he began. The parents flew past him toward the backyard. Henry raced ahead.

He could hear Arthur laughing as he reached for the handle of the back door. When Henry got through the door, Richard was on the ground. A dark-haired child pinned him down while pummeling his crying, submissive opponent.

"Get off of him!" Henry ordered. The dark-haired boy paused just briefly to look up at the newcomer. Henry grabbed hold of Richard and pulled him out from under the other boy. He clutched his son close to his chest.

Arthur took a step in the direction of the door. He lifted an eyebrow in challenge. Henry shot him down with a glare. If his eyes were lasers, Arthur would have been cut in two where he stood.

"Stay away," Henry warned. He had his hands full, but he'd move Arthur out of the way if necessary, though seeing him punch someone might have added to the trauma. Richard did not need to witness any more violence.

"Mama! *MAMA!*" Richard cried. Tears flowed down his cheeks.

"I'm taking you to your mom." Henry carried Richard inside. Richard clung to Henry tighter all the while wailing for his mother.

Elizabeth met them in the living room while Duncan looked on. "Oh, my poor angel."

Richard pulled away from Henry and arched toward her voice. "Mama!" He stretched out his arms to her.

Henry transferred Richard into Elizabeth's arms. "There's where you belong," he cooed.

She rubbed her son's back and rocked him gently. Elizabeth kissed the crown of Richard's head. She tucked him under her chin. His whole body heaved with labored breaths, but the work seemed all in vain. He was not getting enough air in his lungs. "Angel, I know you are upset and hurt, but you need to breathe," Elizabeth directed. After several moments Richard calmed sufficiently for her to sit with him on the couch.

"What happened, angel?" Elizabeth inquired.

"Tommy knocked me down and put dirt in my face." Richard sniffled. "Tommy 'it me."

"You need to learn to fight back, buddy," Duncan admonished.

"And get beaten by Arthur instead?" Elizabeth scoffed.

Duncan huffed. "You always see the worst in him," he chided.

"Richard's here, what, an hour? Look at what happened to him!" She angled so Duncan could see Richard's face. The dirt streaked with Richard's tears.

"Boys will be boys." Duncan shrugged.

"That is bull and you know it," Elizabeth charged. "Arthur instigated it."

"You can't prove that," Duncan countered.

"He didn't rush in here, did he?" Henry threw back.

"Would you listen to him if he had?" Duncan challenged.

"I heard enough: Arthur was laughing," Henry accused.

"You and Arthur don't get along, so how can you be expected to give the impartial facts?" Duncan retorted.

"Sounds like Arthur to me." Elizabeth's upper lip curled back.

"You're not even going to pretend to give him the benefit of the doubt?" Duncan frowned.

"Arthur can go to hell," she snapped.

"I admire your maternal protective urges, but isn't that harsh?" Duncan replied.

"He took a box cutter to my baby, and I will never forget that," Elizabeth argued.

"He made a huge mistake," Duncan acknowledged.

"A mistake?" Henry snarled. "He committed a crime. Give me one good reason he's not in prison for attempted murder."

"You have no clue what you are talking about." Duncan shook his head.

"I heard he spent a week in the hospital," Henry replied.

"It seems my daughter is telling stories." Duncan's gaze

landed on Elizabeth. She straightened and brought Richard closer.

"No, Oliver told me," Henry replied.

"Killing Richard wasn't Arthur's intention," Duncan pronounced.

Henry rolled his eyes. "Because he said so."

Duncan put his hands on his hips. "Richard is my heir. Arthur wouldn't take him from me."

"When are you going to take off your rose-colored glasses and see the real Arthur?" Elizabeth rocked her son.

"How long are you going to keep punishing him?" Duncan inquired.

"What punishment? He wasn't even arrested." Her brow furrowed.

"Six months is a long time for a father to go without seeing his child," Duncan asserted.

"Try five years," Henry muttered.

"I didn't quite catch that," Duncan challenged.

Henry narrowed his eyes in Duncan's direction. "You heard me." Henry's ocean eyes battled Duncan's brown orbs. Neither man backed down.

Realizing the potential for this escalating, Elizabeth tugged on the hem of Henry's shirt. Henry relaxed slightly at her feathery touch.

She locked eyes with her father. "You didn't have to do this, not for Arthur."

"I will not allow you to steal my grandson from me," Duncan said.

"I let you see Richard anytime you want!" Elizabeth returned. "I called you to arrange dinner. How many times have I shuffled plans around just so you could have lunch with him?"

"You never brought him by the mansion," Duncan pointed out.

"Because this is not a safe place for him!" she answered.

"You didn't let Arthur visit with Richard when he came by," Duncan charged.

Elizabeth rolled her eyes. "I have a very good reason for not allowing that: Richard hadn't seen Arthur since he nearly *killed* him."

She got to her feet. Henry fell in line beside her, and they marched to the entry room. Two armed men awaited them at the door.

Elizabeth readjusted Richard's weight to her hip. She turned helpless eyes to Henry. He took her by the waist and brought them close.

"Where do you think you are running off to?" Duncan inquired. They turned around and faced him as a unit. "There's more on the back door, so don't get any ideas," Duncan suggested.

Henry spoke for them. "We're just here for Richard. All we want to do is take him home."

"He is home," Duncan asserted.

Elizabeth jaw dropped. "Are you serious?"

"Your bags are waiting for you in your rooms," Duncan stated, as if that was the end of the discussion.

Elizabeth turned on her heels and marched out of the room.

"Lizzie," Duncan called after her.

Elizabeth didn't slow down. Henry began to follow her out.

"Where are you going?" Duncan questioned.

"With them," Henry snapped. He heard her stomp up the stairs that led to her wing of the mansion and raced to catch up with them. Elizabeth was already in her room by the time he got upstairs. She sat with Richard on the bed.

"I don't want to stay!" Richard cried.

"I'm so sorry, angel." Elizabeth tried to soothe Richard. Tears were streaming down her own face.

Henry sat next to them. He wrapped an arm around Elizabeth's shoulders.

"I wanna go home!" Richard whimpered.

"I know, I know, I want to go home too," Elizabeth cooed.

Duncan showed up in the doorway. "You can't see it right now, but this is for the best," he began.

Elizabeth turned a cold shoulder to her father.

Seeing Elizabeth wall herself off to his words, Duncan looked between her and Richard. You could almost see the wheels turning in his head as he tried to figure out his next tactic. He craned down to try to catch Richard's eyes, but the boy continued to cry into his mother's shoulder. "Don't you want to live with Granddad again, Ricky?" Duncan asked.

Richard lifted his head. "You could come live in the apartment with us," he sniveled.

"But this is our home," Duncan cooed.

"No! T'is bad place! I want live apartment," Richard screamed, tears slurring his words.

Duncan frowned. Richard wasn't usually this resistant.

Henry shot up and placed himself between his family and Duncan.

"You have already done enough damage," Henry growled.

"I am trying to explain things to my daughter," Duncan

argued.

Henry stood firm like a wall. "Not a good time. Richard is in the middle of a meltdown thanks to you," he said.

"He's a child," Duncan replied.

"A highly traumatized child," Henry corrected him. "If you cared about his mental health at all, you wouldn't keep him trapped with his attacker."

"Arthur is his father," Duncan argued.

Henry bit down on his tongue hard. His tattle tale forehead vein popped out.

Duncan held in a smirk. That hit a nerve.

Henry took a moment to collect himself. He blew out a breath. "It's in Richard and Elizabeth's best interest to be away from him."

"And let them be with you?" Duncan raised an eyebrow.

"I'll treat them a hell of a lot better than he does," Henry vowed.

"My daughter and grandson are staying with me," Duncan insisted. "You, on the other hand ..." His lips twisted into a polite if gloating smile. As contempt filled his eyes, the glint in them told another story. "You are free to go anytime you want," Duncan finished.

"If Elizabeth and Richard are stuck here, then so am I," Henry pronounced. "And I'm done being discreet." He slammed the door in Duncan's face and returned to his spot on the bed beside Elizabeth. She leaned into his shoulder.

He laid his cheek on her hair. "We will figure something out," he vowed. There were a thousand more things, a thousand promises that Henry wanted to give her, but right now that was the only one that he could keep.

They sat there until Richard stopped crying. He sagged

against his mother's chest and then became deathly still.

"Are you OK?" Elizabeth pulled back to get a good look at him. Both parents studied him carefully. Richard remained silent but turned his eyes to the luggage that sat in the middle of the room. "What is it, angel?" Elizabeth inquired.

"Where's Lucy?" Richard sniffled.

"Let's see if she's in one of the bags." Henry pushed himself off the bed and headed for the mountain. He unzipped the first suitcase that he got his hands on and began to dig through the clothes. Moving the silks and cotton garments around, he found no Lucy. Where was that bear? The last thing Richard needed was to lose his teddy bear on top of everything else. Henry set the suitcase aside and then went on to the next bag. Unzipping the duffel bag, Henry found it full of bottles of lotions and shampoos—toiletries, mostly plastic and cold. That bag a bust, he laid the biggest suitcase down. Henry flipped the flap open. There squished into the top was a yellow teddy bear. Henry pulled the bear free and let out a grateful sigh. He fluffed out the yellow fur. "Here she is." Henry sat back down in his place on the bed. He handed Lucy over to Richard.

"T'ank you," Richard said rather sedately. Over his head, his parents shared a worried glance. Richard hugged Lucy but hissed when the bear brushed against his cheek.

"Where does it hurt?" Elizabeth began to fuss over Richard.

"My face ouwie," Richard answered.

"Is it bad?" Henry asked.

"Come on, angel. Let's get you cleaned up." Elizabeth carried him into the attached bathroom.

Henry followed. Leaning against the doorframe he

watched Elizabeth set Richard on the countertop. She got a washcloth from a cabinet and started the taps in the sink. Elizabeth held the cloth under the running water and then wrung it out. She brushed the hair out of Richard's face. The removal of the dirt revealed several bruises and a cut lip.

"You are not going to be 'playing' with Tommy anymore," Henry insisted.

Elizabeth nodded in agreement. She caught Richard's eyes. "You hear that?"

"Yes, Mama," Richard replied.

"Henry, could you grab me the duffel bag, please?" Elizabeth requested.

"Sure thing." Henry ducked out and then came right back with the requested bag.

"Arms up," she directed. Richard lifted his arms. Elizabeth fished out a tube of cream and squeezed some out onto her fingertips. Its peppermint scent wafted up into Richard's nostrils. Richard's face scrunched up. He waved his hand under his nose in protest. "It's stinky, Mama."

"I'm sorry. I know you hate the smell, but it will help the bruises go away faster," Elizabeth coaxed. She rubbed some into his cheeks and then upper shoulders. "There. All done." Elizabeth handed him his shirt.

Richard struggled with it momentarily but got it over his head. He slid his arms through.

"Henry and I need to talk for a little bit, OK?" Elizabeth explained. Richard nodded.

A yellow rectangle caught her attention out of the corner of her eye. A pad of paper sat on top of her desk. "Why don't you and Lucy practice your letters at the desk?" she suggested.

Elizabeth sat Richard in the desk chair. She placed Lucy on

top of the desk. Elizabeth dug a pencil out of the top drawer and handed it to him.

Richard wrapped his small fingers around the pencil. "Like this, Mama?" he showed her their positions.

"Yeah," she said.

Henry kissed the crown of Richard's head. "We'll be right back," he promised.

Henry and Elizabeth reentered the bathroom, leaving Lucy to keep watch over her charge. They talked in low tones so they could keep the door open.

"Have they fixed that part of the fence I used to sneak in through?" Henry inquired. The guards on the gate weren't going to let them out even if they could get to the car.

"Running won't do any good. He'll send people after us and take Richard again." Elizabeth wiped her eyes.

"That is kidnapping." Henry raked his fingers through his hair.

"Watch him turn on the charm for one of his friends and chalk it all up to a family squabble." She forced through an obviously fake smile only to drop it. "No one wants to waste resources on that."

"Sounds nauseating," he replied, looking her over, concerned.

"He's got plenty of friends. When one gets suspicious, he'll move on to the next politician he backed—not to mention his ties in South America." She shivered at the last group. Elizabeth held her elbows. "You didn't correct him," she noted.

"Did you expect me to?" Henry asked, reading in between the lines.

"As angry as I am, I'm surprised I held it in," she

answered.

"I don't want Richard seeing me angry when I tell him about being his father," Henry replied.

"Dad wasn't in a place to accept it either." Elizabeth nodded.

He frowned. "How long before he cools down enough? A month?"

She shrugged. "I'm beginning to think hostile is his permanent disposition."

"Well, we can't just sit here," Henry said.

"Waiting is our only option right now," Elizabeth argued. "Maybe if he feels we're cooperative he'll loosen the leash again." She couldn't quite look him in the face.

"Duncan doesn't have the right to treat you like this," he protested.

"It is what it is. We're playthings to him, not people," Elizabeth lamented.

"You and Richard are so much more than that." Henry hooked a crooked finger under her jaw. He brought her eyes to his. "I am not going anywhere without you," Henry promised. "You know that, right?"

"Yeah, but it's nice to hear it." She batted her eyes at him. He drew his thumb over her chin. Henry focused on her mouth. He dipped in while she pushed up on her toes.

Just as they were about to kiss, Richard called from the other room, "Mama!"

Elizabeth patted Henry's chest. "Coming." Henry and she shared a chuckle before returning to the room.

"I finished." Richard displayed a page of barely legible scrawl.

Elizabeth mussed his hair. "That's wonderful!"

"Great job!" Henry added. He smiled at the two most important people in his world. There had to be a way to get his family out of there.

Chapter Eight

Duncan straightened his tie, using his dressing mirror. He critically inspected his image. Duncan pursed his lips. "No," he muttered with a shake of his head. This one didn't cut it. Duncan loosened the tie. He pulled it out from underneath his shirt collar and tossed it aside. His fingertips trailed along the third rung of silk ties on his large rack. He picked out a darker hue of blue. After he was satisfied with the knot, Duncan retrieved the jacket that completed his suit and tugged it on. He buttoned the top button. The garment fit him like a glove—as it should; all his suits were custom made. Ready for the day, he threw open his double doors. They echoed through the bedroom suite, the sound bouncing off his massive four-post bed and other large pieces of furniture. He left the suite and headed down the massive hallway that connected his master wing to the rest of the house.

He went toward the dining room for breakfast. Silvia and Tom sat together across from Arthur. The chair at the head of the table remained reserved for the master of the house.

Arthur sipped on his coffee while reading the paper. Silvia cut Tom's waffle.

"Good morning," Arthur greeted at Duncan's entry.

"Morning." Duncan tipped his head. He came to the table. "Where are Liz and Ricky?" Duncan lowered himself into the head chair.

"I heard they were awake, but I haven't seen them," Arthur answered.

"You haven't checked to see if they're coming for breakfast?" Duncan frowned.

Arthur shrugged. "They'll get hungry eventually."

The butler brought out Duncan's coffee and breakfast.

"Has my daughter come out from her room?" Duncan picked up his utensils.

"Yes, sir. She's been downstairs," the butler answered.

"And where is she now?" Duncan inquired.

"They requested to have their meal on the patio," the butler answered.

Duncan nodded. "That's fine, Felix. My grandson needs to eat."

Felix nodded, not letting on that he would have gotten them food even if Duncan had objected.

"I want more cocoa milk, Mommy," Tom insisted.

"You already drank your milk. Eat your waffle," she directed.

Tom crossed his arms over his chest. "I'm full."

"But you barely touched your food. Don't you want the apples? You like apples," Silvia reminded him.

"I'm full," Tom repeated.

"All right, then it's time to get you dressed." She set her fork down. Silvia wiped her mouth with a napkin as she rose.

She offered her hand out to Tom. "Come along." Tom took her hand as she led him out.

Several minutes of quiet passed between the men. Their forks clunked against their plates as they cut through the food. Arthur looked over at Duncan. His mentor kept his focus on the food in front of him. "Am I still in trouble for last night?" Arthur asked.

Duncan swallowed his current mouthful before speaking. "I'll forgive your slowness in stepping in, but I'm not sure Liz will," he answered.

"Henry came out of nowhere," Arthur remarked.

"And added a healthy layer of polish to his shining armor." Duncan played along for a moment. He debated giving Arthur enough rope to hang himself. There was no time to play this morning. "Still they were under your supervision." Duncan cut off a piece of sausage and ate it.

"I get that," Arthur acknowledged.

"You've made everything with Liz a lot harder than it had to be." Duncan closed his eyes.

Arthur tilted his head and tugged at his earlobe. "I can't do anything but apologize."

"You've got some serious kissing up to do," Duncan noted.

"We're also in the middle of negotiations," Arthur replied. "I think they require my focus."

"Find time to do both. It's not that hard," Duncan directed. "I can tell you exactly what Henry and Elizabeth have been up to for the past few days."

"He's been out less than a week—nothing can heat up that fast." Arthur poured some more syrup on his waffle.

"Maybe with someone she didn't have history with,"

Duncan countered.

"He doesn't have much with the kid," Arthur argued.

"Yet. Don't you care that your wife is basically gift wrapping your son for another man? Elizabeth is offering Richard to Henry on a silver platter," Duncan charged. "And he's eating it up with a spoon."

"He knows the truth." Arthur shifted in his seat.

Duncan had to chuckle at the irony in Arthur's statement. "That he does, but he's been craving family since Grace died," he countered.

Arthur tilted his head. His eyes gleamed in curiosity.

"What?" Duncan frowned.

"You called his mother by her name again," Arthur noted.

Duncan went along as if Arthur hadn't said anything. "Even if he wasn't into a kid—which he is—how could anyone not love that grandson of mine? Elizabeth knows how to pull on Henry's heartstrings. You should have seen his eyes last night: he was ready to chop off my head," Duncan reported.

"Same here." Arthur finished the last bite of food on his plate. He folded the paper up, leaving it on the tabletop. Arthur stood and straightened his suit jacket. Duncan reached over to Arthur's place and took the paper.

"I would have handed you the paper," Arthur remarked.

"I got it," Duncan replied.

"Are we riding in together?" Arthur inquired.

"You go ahead. I'm going to have a talk with my daughter first." Duncan dismissed him, flicking his wrists to open the paper.

Arthur's chest fell. "See you at the office."

―――――――

RESTORATION

Duncan stepped out onto the patio stones as two different sets of laughter rang through the air. Richard sat in Elizabeth's lap. Duncan gathered Henry must have said or done something funny because the laughing he heard came from Elizabeth and Richard. The two were both intently listening to the man sitting at the head of the outdoor table. Henry reached over and mussed up Richard's hair—a familial scene if he had ever seen one.

"Good morning," Duncan greeted.

"Morning, Granddad," Richard replied.

"How are you doing today, Ricky?" Duncan asked.

Richard shrugged. "OK." He stuck his hand in a bowl of mixed berries.

"Use your fork, bud," Duncan directed.

Henry scrunched his face up momentarily. "They're just berries."

Duncan looked at his daughter. "We need to talk."

Elizabeth rolled her eyes at the intruder and, instead of engaging him, focused on Richard. "Would you like another waffle?" she asked her son.

"No, t'ank you," Richard answered.

"I'm not going to disappear," Duncan asserted.

"Are you full?" Elizabeth inquired. Richard nodded and then looked back at her.

"You got your stubbornness from your mother," Duncan pronounced.

Elizabeth caught Richard's eyes. "Why don't you go play, baby?"

"OK," Richard reluctantly agreed.

"Stay where I can see you," she instructed. "And leave the pool alone, OK?"

"Yes, Mama," Richard replied. Elizabeth kissed his forehead and set him on his feet.

He scampered off to the patch of green just out of earshot.

Duncan raised an eyebrow. "Do you really think this is going to go that badly?"

"Richard heard enough last night." Henry took up his juice glass.

"Does he speak for you now?" Duncan motioned his head toward Henry.

Elizabeth looked at Henry. "She's not interested in speaking with you herself," Henry said.

"Lizzie, you are acting like a child," Duncan reprimanded.

"You refuse to treat her like an adult," Henry countered.

"What is this attitude of yours teaching Ricky? Your melancholy is rubbing off on him," Duncan replied.

"You gave him a taste of freedom and then you took it away," Henry accused. "Did you think he'd be happy to have his footing ripped out from under him?"

"How can you take him back so quickly after he's been who-knows-where for five years?" Duncan charged.

"You knew damn well where I was!" he challenged.

"That's a heavy accusation." Duncan put his hands on his hips.

Henry sneered. "Your lap dog wouldn't make those kinds of moves without at least getting your approval."

"Arthur is very loyal." Duncan puffed out his chest.

"You wanted me gone. Did you tell Arthur to make me go away?" Henry questioned.

"I merely suggested that he needed to secure his position as Richard's father before you usurped him," Duncan replied.

"He's the usurper!" Henry snapped.

RESTORATION

"I can see how you would see it that way: you asked Lizzie to marry you first." Duncan rubbed his chin. "Richard would be your son if you'd had your way."

Henry narrowed his eyes trying to get a read on the man in front of him. Something just didn't match up here. While Duncan's facial expressions synced up with his words, his eyes radiated a warning. Saying the wrong thing could land them in a trap. Henry weighed his words.

"Damn straight I wish she had married me instead. My feelings for Elizabeth haven't gone away," Henry admitted. Elizabeth placed her hand on his arm.

"She is still legally married," Duncan pointed out.

Henry pursed his lips. "A good lawyer can fix that."

"They have a child together; a lawyer can't erase him," Duncan countered.

"And I wouldn't want him to," Henry returned.

"Isn't Richard the reason you left?" Duncan questioned.

"Don't ever say I balked!" Henry shot up and punched the tabletop with both hands. "I would never walk away from them!"

Duncan looked Henry over. The aggressiveness was new. The years away had changed the young man he had known. He had a new edge to him. Duncan straightened his shoulders. This might bear exploring.

"One moment I was putting Richard into his crib and the next I had a gun to my neck." Henry gestured to the spot.

"Are you actually buying this story?" Duncan questioned.

Elizabeth glared at him. "I was there when the thugs dragged Henry off. I know he didn't go willingly."

"She does have a voice," Duncan taunted.

"Most of the time, I think you'd be happier if I didn't

speak." She crossed her arms over her chest.

"You know I love you, Lizzie," Duncan began.

"Kidnapping is a funny way to show it," Elizabeth retorted.

"One day you'll see," Duncan promised.

"What about my job?" Elizabeth inquired.

"You can keep working," Duncan agreed. The way he bit his cheek and narrowed his eyes told her he'd rather she'd stop. "Do you have anything you're scheduled for today?" Duncan asked.

"No, but I have a fitting tomorrow and a show this weekend," Elizabeth answered.

"When does your campaign for that new fashion house start?"

"Next week," Elizabeth answered.

Duncan nodded his head a few times and changed the subject. "I called Ms. Wallace, and she said she's still willing to tutor Ricky. She'll be by at the usual time."

"Are you going to let us take him out?" Henry asked.

"No, my grandson stays put for now," Duncan said.

"Why?" Henry challenged.

"I can't necessarily say that I trust you. You are technically trespassing in my home after all." Duncan shrugged. He spun around and walked away humming to himself.

"Do you think he'd call the cops on me?" Henry asked.

Elizabeth shook her head. "I doubt it. He won't risk the beat cops actually listening when Richard and I ask to leave with you."

RESTORATION

"Stop!" Duncan whimpered. The whirring of a chainsaw nearly drowned him out. He scrambled away from his attacker on all fours. He raised an arm to shield his face. The chainsaw roared as Henry lifted it over his head. He brought the saw down full force. Blood squirted back up onto his face and clothes.

Henry groaned in his sleep. Elizabeth twirled the feathery ends of his blond spikes around her fingertips. His head rested in her lap. His face began to twitch. She knew he would be waking up soon. Henry restlessly turned over onto his back. His eyes flew open. He began to jump up, but Elizabeth eased him back into her lap.

"Welcome back from dreamland." She smiled. Henry lay still. He allowed his heart to calm.

"How long did I sleep?" Henry rubbed his eyes.

"About a half hour," Elizabeth answered. "You dreamt."

"You could tell?" Henry questioned. He sat up.

"It looked rather … disturbing," she replied.

"You have no idea," Henry replied. "I want to dream about paint again."

"Flashback?" Elizabeth asked.

"No, just a nightmare," Henry replied.

"Was it about Wonder Ridge?" She rubbed his shoulders.

"Not directly." He brought his legs over the side of the couch and leaned back in. "I think you might want to keep weapons out of my hands when I'm around your father," Henry quipped.

"You're not the only one, babe," Elizabeth replied.

Henry snuggled in a little closer to Elizabeth. A move she reciprocated. He offered his palm out to Elizabeth. She laid her hand on top of his. "Sorry I fell asleep," Henry said.

"No worries," Elizabeth replied.

"Thanks to Wonder Ridge, my schedule is totally off whack," he added. She nodded her understanding but kept quiet in hopes he would continue. "Pretty much the only thing to do there was sketch or sleep." Henry stretched.

"What about eating?" Elizabeth inquired.

"The food sucked." He smirked and gave a small laugh.

"I have something I want to show you." She stood, pulling Henry up by their joined hands in the process.

"Where are we going?" Henry inquired.

"Telling would spoil the surprise, wouldn't it?" Elizabeth quipped. She stepped behind him. Elizabeth covered his eyes with her soft hands. "Start walking," she instructed. Her breath tickled his ear.

The two crossed a patch of yard along an inner iron fence. He felt them walk through one door, through a space, and then another door. "OK, now you can open your eyes." Elizabeth pulled back her hands.

Henry found a bare room. It smelled of a fresh coat of primer on the wall. Most of the room had a concrete floor. "Is this the pool house?" Henry questioned.

She nodded. "I figured we could furnish this room out into a studio for you," Elizabeth offered. "What do you think?"

"It's got great light." Henry admired two large windows toward the back of the space.

"Does it get your seal of approval?" Elizabeth inquired.

"Well, it's better than my last studio," he quipped.

"How so?" she questioned.

"This one has air conditioning." Henry smirked. Elizabeth nodded her head with a chuckle. The urge to grab Elizabeth and kiss her senseless in that moment was extremely strong. To fight the temptation, he shoved his hands into the pockets of his jeans.

"You saved my paintings," Henry marveled. Wide-eyed, he made his way to the rack as if drawn by a magnet. His heart broke a little more with each passing painting. Sure they all were his work, and he was grateful to have them back, but there was one that was especially precious to him, and it looked like it wasn't among his surviving works.

Knowing which painting he was looking for, Elizabeth turned him around. She pointed him toward his goal. His old easel set up where the natural light from the large windows hit it at the perfect angle.

Henry pulled the protective cloth off. He stepped back as the removal of the cloth revealed a square canvas portrait Henry had painted of his mother. He wiped the moisture from his eyes. "Thank you," Henry said softly. He raised an eyebrow. "When did you find time to set this up?"

"I made a few calls last night." Elizabeth smirked.

"And got everything here and set up right under my nose in a morning?" he inquired as they walked back to the metal racks.

"Oliver helped me get your studio packed up," she said. "There are some boxes of your things in another room."

"There wasn't much, I imagine," Henry said. He pulled out a medium-sized plastic crate from the bottom shelf of the rack. Henry surveyed its contents. He picked up a cracked tube of scarlet paint. "Well, this one's a goner." Henry frowned. Setting it aside, he dug into the rest of the tubes. Time had not been kind to his paints.

He rubbed his fingers together feeling the residue.

She got a rag down from the shelf. "You could get pretty messy," Elizabeth mused with a smirk.

"And you liked it," Henry deadpanned.

"I loved it," she declared, holding the rag out to him. Elizabeth would often find swatches of a rainbow of colors all over his hand and sometimes on his face. The first time she'd walked in on him painting he'd been elbow deep in it. They locked eyes as he accepted the cloth. She couldn't help wondering, hoping that he was reliving the same memories. "We'll need to get you some new supplies," she said.

Henry sighed. "It's been a long time since I held a paintbrush." He couldn't even bring himself to open the case just yet.

Elizabeth reached out and tugged a hand from his pocket. She entwined their fingers. "I have faith," Elizabeth pronounced.

Henry smiled. He brought their joined hands up to his lips and kissed the back of her knuckles.

"We could put in a play table over here for Richard. That way when you need to be out I can watch him while I work." Henry motioned to an open area.

"Sounds lovely," Elizabeth said. "We could bring the one down from the third-floor playroom. He's too scared to go in there anymore."

"Something happened in there?" Henry asked.

"Yeah." She pressed her lips together.

Taking that as a cue he moved on. "We could move more of his toys down here. There's more than enough space," Henry offered. His eyes went from twinkling to dull after a thought.

She frowned. "Don't you like it?"

"It's not that." He shook his head.

"Then what is it?" Elizabeth asked.

"I want Richard to know who I am," Henry replied.

"I know, so do I," she agreed.

Henry's shoulders sagged. "But?"

"I know what my father is capable of," Elizabeth said.

They heard small footsteps hitting the concrete floor fast. Richard ran straight to his mother as she pivoted to him. "Hi, angel." Elizabeth beamed.

"Ricky said you might be out here," Jessica said from her spot in the doorway.

"Thank you for coming in," Elizabeth replied.

"Anything for Ricky." Jessica smiled. "Same time tomorrow?" Elizabeth nodded. "See you then."

"Do you like your surprise, Ri?" Richard asked.

"You were in on it, huh?" Henry smirked. "It's great, little prince."

"What's that?" Richard said pointing to the painting on the easel.

Henry walked Richard over to it. He knelt and draped an arm around his son's waist. "This is my mom," Henry explained. He watched his son's face light up.

"She's pretty," Richard remarked.

Chapter Nine

Henry hung a canvas on his easel. Richard made soft vrooming sounds as he played with Hot Wheels cars on his relocated play table. Henry consulted his sketch pad. He had it turned over to the drawing he was going to paint from. Henry picked up a palette knife and set to mixing a cerulean blue. "How you doing, bud?" he asked.

Richard raised one hand with a thumbs-up sign. "Good."

He picked up a paintbrush and dipped the tip in. His hand started to shake. Henry wrapped his free hand around his wrist to support the hand, but the tremors didn't stop. Suddenly his mind went completely blank. He couldn't remember where the color was supposed to go. Henry blew out a breath. He closed his eyes trying to bring the project into focus. The tighter Henry squeezed them the fuzzier the image became to him. Finally, it all blurred into one bland color. He set the paintbrush down on the palette. This wasn't working.

"Want to make a picture for Mama?" Henry offered.

"Yeah," Richard agreed.

Henry smiled. "Let's put up your cars, and I'll get you

some paper."

He pulled out several jars of finger paint out of a cubby. "What do you think she would like a picture of?" Henry asked as he twisted the lid off one of them. He lined them up on the table next to the children's easel.

"Fireworks," Richard suggested. "Mama likes fireworks."

"Wow," Henry remarked. "Ambitious. I like it!"

"We saw the fireworks from our roof in July," Richard added.

"Oh, yeah? Cool." Henry smiled. "Was it fun?" He ripped a large piece of paper out of a pad for Richard to use.

"It was loud but fun," Richard answered.

Henry clipped the paper securely to a children's easel. "Are you ready?" Henry asked.

Richard looked down at his outfit. Henry sensed his hesitation. "What's the matter, little prince?" he asked.

Richard hung his head. "Daddy will be mad if I get my clothes dirty."

"You won't get in trouble," Henry promised. He went back to the cubby and grabbed a protective garment. "This is for you." Henry handed a new white T-shirt to Richard. The young boy pulled the oversized shirt over his clothes. "You can get it as messy as you like," Henry coaxed.

Richard tentatively dipped his fingers into a blue. He dragged the paint over the paper, creating several choppy streaks. Richard giggled, getting more of the same color paint.

"You're a natural," Henry encouraged. "How about another color?" He held a rag for Richard to wipe off his fingers.

"Yeah!" Richard cleaned off his hands. He chose red to continue. Richard went on through the other paints until the large paper was filled with colors. "Done," he pronounced.

"Now it's time to sign it," Henry said.

"Sign it?" Richard questioned.

"Do you know how to write your name?" Henry inquired.

"No." Richard shook his head.

"You know how to write your letters, right? I saw you write them," Henry coached.

"I do." Richard nodded.

"OK, I'll tell you how to spell your name, and you can write the letters. How does that sound? You think we can do that?" Henry offered.

"I'll try," Richard agreed.

"R." Henry steadied Richard's hand guiding him to make the shape of the letter. "Great job!" He wiped off Richard's finger and then dipped it into another container. "Now the I," Henry coaxed. They got onto the third letter before a knock on the side door.

"Stay put. I will be right back," Henry promised. He crossed the room.

Henry opened the side door to find Duncan standing there.

"Elizabeth isn't here. She had a meeting after her fitting." Henry hoped he could cut Duncan off at the pass.

"She left my grandson with you," Duncan noted. He could hear Richard's laughter from inside.

Henry refrained from rolling his eyes. "Richard is fine."

"I would like to see that for myself," Duncan insisted.

"Shouldn't you be at work or something?" Henry frowned.

Duncan smirked. "I'm the boss. I make my own hours." He gazed expectantly at Henry. The younger man returned a flat-faced stare. "Aren't you going to let me in?" Duncan inquired.

Henry peeked outside, looking left and then right. Once he was satisfied Duncan was alone, Henry stepped aside and let him into the room. He swiftly closed the door after Duncan stepped inside.

Duncan scanned the room. "You're certainly making yourself at home," he remarked. Grace's portrait hung in a prominent spot on a wall.

"I prefer things at the penthouse, but we'll make do," Henry replied.

"I could set you up in one," Duncan offered.

Henry smirked. "I can't be bought."

"Luckily for me, there are other options." Duncan left what they were unsaid.

"If you really want me gone there's an easy way to get me out of your hair, let Elizabeth and Richard leave and I'll go with them," Henry offered.

"I wouldn't be so cocky if I were in your shoes," Duncan challenged.

"Look who's here, little prince," Henry called.

Richard peeked around his picture. He waved his paint-covered hands in the air. Duncan walked over to the kid's easel. He carefully hugged the boy, mindful that he didn't want to get paint on his own clothes.

"We're making a present for Mama!" Richard announced.

"I see that." Duncan smiled. He looked at the swirls of color, not able to make heads or tails of the piece, but painting never had appealed to him. "Are you at a stopping point? It's getting a bit late for lunch," Duncan said.

"We already ate," Henry informed him.

"Is that right?" Duncan inquired.

Richard patted his stomach leaving a perfect handprint on the T-shirt. "We had a big lunch," he reported.

"What did you eat?" Duncan asked.

"C'icken and broccoli, o and rice," Richard answered.

"He mostly ate the rice," Henry noted.

Duncan's eyebrows raised in surprise.

Henry rolled his eyes. "I know I need to feed him."

"Of course," Duncan replied.

"I'm sure they need you at the office. I can take care of Richard," Henry asserted. He took his place next to Richard, turning his back to Duncan.

Duncan frowned. Had Henry just dismissed him?

"Ready to finish writing your name?" Henry turned his full attention to Richard. Duncan could see himself out.

Duncan stopped. He looked in the picture window while Henry's attention was focused on Richard. Duncan watched them laugh together. Henry turned and grinned at Richard. Richard smiled at him in return. There was an ease between the two that Duncan hadn't seen between Richard and Arthur.

Henry felt someone watching them. He lifted his eyes to the window. Duncan acknowledged him with a look and then followed the trail out of the mansion.

"Come on, let's wash our hands, and then you can get back to playing with your toys." Henry brought Richard over to the sink and turned on the water.

Henry stared at the canvas. He could hear each fiber laughing at him. There was another knock at the door. Henry went to the door thankful for the distraction.

He found the butler waiting for him. "Mr. Tate is on the phone for you." Felix motioned to the phone in the room.

"Thank you, Felix." Henry tipped his head.

"If I can be of any help at all, please, let me know." Felix nodded before leaving.

Henry grabbed the receiver off the phone base hanging on the wall. "Hi, Ollie."

"I went over to the penthouse and it's empty," Oliver reported. "What happened?"

"Duncan happened." Henry clenched his jaw.

"What did he pull this time?" Oliver groaned.

"I think you already have some idea." Henry sighed. "He snatched Richard from a tutoring session."

"What the hell!" Oliver interjected. Henry could almost see his friend pinching the bridge of his nose. "Is Richard OK?" Oliver asked.

"He's calming down, but we are with him," Henry answered.

"OK, that's good," Oliver said.

"Anyway, we'll be stuck at the mansion for a while: Duncan and his guards won't let us take Richard off the property," Henry added.

"Seriously?" Oliver groaned. "OK, after the table read, I'll be heading over and we'll put together some escape plans."

"You're welcome over, but Elizabeth won't run," Henry informed him.

"This can't fly," Oliver objected.

"This scare kind of put the fear of God in her." Henry leaned against the wall.

"Duncan likes to keep her under his thumb." Oliver sighed.

"Can't say I don't share her fears. Duncan's no stranger to using kids as pawns against their parents," Henry answered.

"His own grandson?" Oliver questioned.

"His own daughter," Henry remarked. "He pulled some despicable moves on Victoria during her first divorce attempt."

"Using Liz?" Oliver questioned.

"That's her story to tell," Henry replied.

Oliver rubbed his forehead. "OK, well, I'll be over and we'll brainstorm. There has to be something we can do."

―――――

Elizabeth checked her hair and makeup in the rearview mirror before exiting her car. She was going into this meeting looking every inch the supermodel that she was. Elizabeth glanced through the glass front of the bar where Serena had arranged the meeting. She spotted Serena at the far end of the bar. Sitting beside her on the counter was a stack of four sketch pads. The blonde turned her back to the door to order from the bartender. Elizabeth straightened her shoulders and pushed the door open. She crossed the room to her. Elizabeth announced her presence. "Ms. Wilson."

Serena spun on her stool. She looked around to see if anyone had come with Elizabeth. The blonde didn't even try to hide her disappointment when she realized neither of the guys was there.

"Where is Henry?" Serena inquired.

"Bonding with his son." Elizabeth smiled. She motioned to the stack of sketch pads. "Are these his?" Elizabeth asked.

"Yeah," Serena said. "That's all of them." The bartender set her drink down. She spun around and picked it up.

"Thanks, I'll get them directly to him." Elizabeth reached for the books.

Serena leaned in and blocked Elizabeth's path. "How can I reach Henry?" Serena inquired.

"You've done your good deed. Now, can't you just leave Henry alone?" Elizabeth questioned.

"This wasn't an unselfish move," Serena admitted. "Henry and I need to talk."

"Henry's made it clear he does not want to see you," Elizabeth stated.

"It's important." Serena pursed her lips.

"If you're trying to say something, spit it out." Elizabeth put her hands on her hips.

"It's between me and him, OK?" Serena snapped.

"I don't have the time or the energy for not-so-subtle implications. Say it or hold your piece," Elizabeth said.

"I think Henry should be the first to know," Serena countered.

"Whoever put you up to this should get their money back." Elizabeth rolled her eyes.

"Nobody's paying me anything or ..." Serena began.

"Henry has a family," Elizabeth asserted. "He just got us back. I don't think he'd appreciate you trumping all of this up to pull us apart." She reached into her purse and pulled out a Polaroid that Oliver had taken of them during their visit to the penthouse. Elizabeth let Serena get a good look at it. "We are a real family." In the pic, the trio cuddled together on the couch. Elizabeth on one side of Richard and Henry on the other, all bright, smiling faces. Henry smiled the biggest of the three. "Now if you'll excuse me, Henry is expecting me at home." She stuffed the picture back in her purse.

"How do you know he's not just in it for the kid?" Serena challenged.

Elizabeth arched an eyebrow and tilted her head. She crossed her arms over her chest. Elizabeth wasn't going to dignify the question with an answer.

Elizabeth pushed past Serena and picked up the stack of books. A loose page fell to the floor. Elizabeth slid the stack back into its place on the bar. She picked up the paper, becoming transfixed on the image of a one-year-old: a total ringer for her son at that age. The whole world fell away. Elizabeth's hand groped for a stool. She sat, never taking her eyes off the paper. The drawing looked like a black-and-white photograph. This level of detail—it must have taken Henry at least a full day to draw.

She turned the page over and found Henry's handwriting. The date he wrote in an upper corner corresponded to the day Richard turned a year old. Elizabeth began to read the note Henry had written on the bottom:

Happy birthday, Richard. Daddy loves you very much.

Elizabeth's eyes brimmed with tears. They blurred the words. She wiped her eyes. Elizabeth lifted the cover of the top book and slid the paper inside. She figured it was better she didn't read anymore. The message was meant for Richard.

———

Elizabeth fingered the edges of another one of Henry's special drawings where it sat on top of her low dresser. As transfixed as she had become she still sensed Henry come up from behind. He wrapped his arms around her.

RESTORATION

"Have I mentioned I want this one framed too?" Elizabeth said. He kissed the shoulder that her charmeuse strap left bare. She'd opted for something a little showier than the PJs she had been wearing to sleep. From the way, Henry's hungry eyes roamed over her in the mirror it had been the right choice. Elizabeth smirked. She melted back into him.

"You can frame as many of those as you wish," Henry promised.

"How did your first daddy day go?" Elizabeth turned down the covers.

"Great," he replied. In his heart, he longed for Richard to call him that.

"Did you get any painting done?" She fluffed her pillow.

He shook his head, thinking about the bare canvas still hanging on the easel. "I mixed some paint, but …" Henry trailed off with a pained look on his face. He let her go. Elizabeth went over to the bed.

"It's a start," Elizabeth said. "Baby steps."

"Right," he agreed.

He turned off the overhead light. She slid into bed, leaving a lamp on for Henry to find his way. He joined her shortly.

"Penny for your thoughts," Elizabeth coaxed.

Henry pushed himself up on his elbow. "I've been thinking if things were different. I would want us to have another; kid, I mean."

Her face brightened considerably. "Really?" She batted her eyelashes.

"After today how could I not? Richard's pretty terrific. You've done a wonderful job with him."

"I can't take all the credit. I know where he got his gentle spirit from," Elizabeth replied.

"This is a little premature. We haven't even said we're officially getting back together yet never mind— we haven't even talked about …" His voice trailed off as he tried not to blush.

"Well, we are sharing a bed." She blushed.

"True." Henry chuckled. He lifted his hand and cupped her cheek. She smiled into his palm. "You are so beautiful," Henry marveled.

He locked eyes with her as if he was asking for permission. Elizabeth inched forward. Henry met her halfway. He gently brushed his lips against hers. She tilted her head and went in for a deeper kiss. Elizabeth placed a hand on Henry's chest to urge him to his back.

Just as things were getting heated, Arthur's booming voice came from down the hall. "What the hell?" Henry muttered. Elizabeth let him get up. He charged out the door.

"What are you doing out of bed!" Arthur thundered.

Richard began to tremble at Arthur's volume. "Leave him alone!" he heard Henry's voice order. Before Richard knew it, big strong hands scooped him up from behind. Without another word, Henry turned around and headed toward Elizabeth's and his bedroom.

He carried Richard directly to the attached bathroom and then set him on his feet. It was too late. His pajama shorts were already wet. Tears welled in Richard's eyes. "I didn't mean to."

"It's OK," Henry said.

"I'm sorry," Richard sobbed.

Henry locked eyes with his son, "I am not mad at you, OK? Neither is your mom." He rubbed Richard's shoulders comfortingly.

"That's right." Elizabeth came and knelt down beside

them.

"Now your mom is going to get you in the shower while I get you some clean PJs? Does that sound all right?" Henry asked.

Richard sniffled but nodded his head. Henry cradled the back of Richard's neck in the palm of one hand and kissed Richard's forehead. "It's going to be OK," he encouraged. "I'll be right back."

Henry made it into Richard's room in a flash. He turned on the light. Henry grabbed Lucy from off the bed and then crossed over to the dresser. He pulled the top drawer out and surveyed its contents. Henry grabbed what Richard would need out of it and went on to the second drawer where he found Richard's pajamas. He picked out the softest set he could find.

The temperature went down ten degrees. Henry didn't have to turn around to know that someone was in the room with him.

"It's not funny to stop a little kid from getting to the bathroom," Henry asserted.

"He shouldn't have been out of bed." Arthur sneered.

"You need to stay out of my face," Henry growled. "Why don't you rein your own brat in and leave my son to me?" Henry snapped. He shoved the drawer closed rather forcefully.

"Temper, temper," Arthur taunted.

"Get out of our wing!" Henry thundered. He clipped Arthur's shoulder on the way out of the room.

Henry stomped back down to their room. The shower running told him they were still in the bathroom. He locked the door behind him. Henry leveraged a chair under the doorknob for good measure. He closed his eyes and took a deep breath. Henry counted to ten before blowing the air out. He needed to shake his anger at Arthur before rejoining his family. Henry put a smile on his face and as he heard the water cut off. The door muffled their conversation until he stepped closer.

"Only babies wet their pants," Richard said.

"You are not a baby," Elizabeth corrected lovingly as she dried him with a towel. "Henry doesn't think so either. We know you were trying, angel."

Henry knocked on the doorframe. "Here you go." He presented the clothes. "I hope these will work."

Elizabeth reached out and took the clothes. "All right, let's get you dressed." She turned to her son.

Elizabeth helped Richard steady himself while he got on his underwear and sleep shorts. "All better," she pronounced. They brought him back into the bedroom. Richard picked Lucy up from the bed where Henry had set her.

"Do I gotta go to my room?" Richard asked.

Henry shook his head. "I think you should sleep in here with us tonight."

"OK," Richard agreed readily.

"C'mere." Henry lifted Richard into the middle of the bed. Elizabeth switched the lights off before joining them. The trio got under the comforter and settled in for the night. Richard did his best to stay still, but he couldn't sleep. Henry sensed his restlessness. He began to hum a lullaby. Softly, the humming became singing. Richard closed his eyes. His father's voice lulled him to sleep.

Chapter Ten

R ichard froze. Arthur loomed larger than life in front of him in the living room. Henry and Elizabeth entered the room a moment after their son. Henry picked Richard up and settled him on his hip farthest from Arthur.

"Not a word," he warned. Henry reached behind him and grabbed Elizabeth's hand in his free one. He led past Arthur, leaving him behind with a parting glare.

Henry ushered his family inside the pool house. He set Richard down and closed the door. Henry locked it and then leaned against the door. Henry inhaled, grateful they had a little hideaway at least in this place. Workdays stuck at the estate were tolerable with Arthur and Duncan at the production studio's office. Henry could foresee weekends, and other days Arthur had off, would be a problem. If they kept tripping over each other like yesterday, he was going to snap. Henry sighed.

"What do you want to play with first?" Elizabeth asked.

"Trains." Richard batted his eyes.

Elizabeth got the bin of trains and tracks out of a cubby.

Henry pushed off the door and looked around the room. The canvas he had set up still hung on the easel, mocking him. Still empty. Instead of tackling it, Henry went to retrieve the last couple of boxes of his things from an inner room. He brought them back and set them on the floor. Henry retrieved an artist's knife from his bag of tools. He sliced tape on the first box. He pulled the flaps apart to find a stack of clothing.

"I found my old painting shirts," he informed Elizabeth.

She looked up from where she sat on the play rug with Richard. "Excellent," she replied. "We'll have to have them washed before you wear them."

"Yeah." Henry wrinkled up his nose at the musty smell. Henry lifted the clothes out to see if there was anything else in the box. Under all the garments lay a smaller, plastic, protective box. Henry brought it out. He flipped it over to examine all the sides. Henry popped the lid off and set it aside on top of the clothes. "My glove." He smiled at the contents.

"I think Oliver packed that one," Elizabeth said.

"Look at this, little prince," Henry beckoned. He pounded his hand into the aged leather. It needed a little oil, but otherwise it was in good condition. Richard set aside his train and came closer. He titled his head to get a good look. "It's a baseball mitt," Henry explained.

"Baseball?" Richard asked.

"It's a game. I played in high school," Henry began to answer the implied question. "It's kind of like catch."

"I've never played catch," Richard said.

"You haven't played catch? Every kid should know how to play catch," Henry said. Richard looked at the ground. "I'll teach you," Henry promised.

"What do you say we go out and throw the ball around after lunch?" Henry offered.

Someone knocked on the door. Henry answered it.

"It's me again," Duncan said.

Elizabeth dropped a kiss on the crown of Richard's head before pushing herself up onto her feet. She joined Henry at the door. "Hi, Dad," Elizabeth greeted.

"I'm here to extend a lunch invitation," Duncan replied. Elizabeth and Henry exchanged glances. "For all of you," Duncan added.

"We were going to eat out—" she began.

"Here," Duncan finished for her. "Arthur is out for a business lunch, and Silvia took Tom to the park for a picnic."

"You're asking us because your preferred company bailed on you?" Elizabeth raised an eyebrow.

"What if I sent them out so I could get you to eat with me?" Duncan insisted. "Can't a father want to share a meal with his daughter?"

"Normal fathers," Henry quipped.

Duncan rolled his eyes before turning his attention back to Elizabeth. "Spend some time with your old man," he cajoled. Elizabeth straightened her shoulders. She was close to caving. Duncan could see it. "Come on, I've been waiting for you," he said to make her feel guilty.

"I don't know," she replied.

"Why don't we ask Ricky what he would like?" Duncan suggested.

For a moment Henry thought about refusing him entry. Elizabeth patted Henry's shoulder. He stepped aside, clearing the door.

Duncan walked over and craned down to his grandson.

Richard looked up from his train. "You want to eat with your granddad, don't you, Ricky?" Duncan coaxed.

Richard caught Elizabeth's eyes over his granddad's shoulder. She nodded. "OK," Richard said.

Duncan clapped. "That's settled then. Let's go inside." He took Richard by the hand and led him into the main house. "I had the cook make your favorite today." Richard looked back at Elizabeth.

"What is for lunch?" Elizabeth inquired.

"Steak tacos for Ricky, steak for us guys, and steak taco salad for you," Duncan answered.

"Sit next to me," Duncan directed. Richard climbed into the chair to the side of his grandfather. Elizabeth and Henry settled on the other side of Duncan as Felix brought in the first few plates of food.

"How was the show last night?" Duncan asked picking up his fork and knife in a grand fashion.

"Same old, same old—hectic," she said. Felix set her salad in front of her. Elizabeth tilted her head. "Thank you."

"You came home early," he noted as security had told him.

"I didn't feel like going to the after party." Elizabeth shrugged. "I wanted to get home to my baby."

"As any good mother would." Duncan nodded.

"He missed her," Henry pronounced. "Didn't you?" Richard nodded his head.

"I heard you didn't go to Liz's show." Duncan frowned.

"I would have been there in a heartbeat, but someone needed to take care of Ricky," Henry replied.

"That's what Silvia is here for. She is the nanny," Duncan asserted.

Henry looked at him as if he was crazy. "Silvia takes care

of Tom."

"So?" Duncan's brow furrowed.

"We don't want a repeat performance of the other night." Henry rubbed his eyes.

"So your solution is to separate them indefinitely?" Duncan scoffed.

"As much as possible," Henry replied.

"Plus we are not going to risk Ricky getting left alone with Arthur," Elizabeth added.

"And the real reason comes out. How is he supposed to repair his relationship with his son if you keep blocking him?"

Richard picked up one of his tacos. He moved to take a bite of it but changed his mind and set it back on the plate. Richard groaned softly. He rubbed his stomach.

"What's wrong, Ricky? You love tacos." Duncan frowned.

"My tummy 'urts," Richard replied.

"Do you feel bad anywhere else?" Elizabeth asked.

"Just my tummy," Richard said.

"Do you feel like you're going to hurl?" she inquired.

"Don't think so." Richard shook his head.

"Well, maybe eating a little will help your tummy feel better," Duncan suggested.

His appetite had been waning since their return to the estate.

"You can go ahead and just eat the cheese and sour cream," Henry coaxed.

Richard picked up his fork and picked out the dairy on top of the tacos.

"May I be excused?" he requested. "I'm tired."

Henry wiped the corner of his mouth with a napkin. "I'll take care of him," he offered. Henry got up and crossed behind

Elizabeth and Duncan. "Come on, little prince." He collected the boy. Father and son walked out of the dining room side by side.

Duncan checked his watch. "It's barely past one. How can he be tired?" he wondered out loud.

"Ricky hasn't been sleeping well," Elizabeth explained. "The nightmares are back."

"He'll grow out of them," Duncan assured her.

She shoved her next bite of salad into her mouth to stop herself from making a retort. "How is Cleo?" Elizabeth asked.

"Fine, she's fine," Duncan answered.

"Is she on an assignment? I haven't seen her since we got back," she continued.

"Cleo quit working when we got married. You know that, Lizzie," he replied. "My wife doesn't need a job."

"Of course not, I just thought she might be doing one of her friends a favor." Elizabeth tilted her head.

"She took her sister to Paris for the week," Duncan said. "She'll be back tonight."

"OK, good," she replied. Maybe that would help him loosen up.

"Who's the photographer for your shoot tomorrow?" Duncan inquired.

"Tristian," Elizabeth answered.

"Tristian ..." Duncan cut another piece off of his steak. "Tristian Grammar?"

"Huh-uh." Elizabeth covered her mouth as she chewed on her bite of salad.

Um, well now. Things just got interesting. This could be entertaining if he played it right. He only wished he could be there when everything shook out. Maybe the aftermath would be satisfying enough. "Isn't he the one that took the shots of you and Ricky for the *Vogue* spread?" Duncan inquired.

"Yes, he is." She nodded.

He paused as if thinking hard. "Why don't you take Ricky with you?"

Elizabeth nearly choked. She took a drink of water. "You'll let us take him out?" Elizabeth asked for clarification.

"This doesn't mean all the time. I am making an exception for tomorrow," Duncan said. She nodded. "We might have to set some ground rules," he added.

"We'll want to take him out to lunch and dinner," Elizabeth said.

"All right," Duncan agreed. Her eyes widened in surprise. "I can be reasonable," Duncan said, going back to his food. "You'll have to have him back before his bedtime," he insisted. "I won't budge on that."

"He needs his sleep," Elizabeth agreed.

"He's a growing boy." Duncan nodded.

Henry lay on the bed holding Richard until the boy fell asleep. He sensed Richard's breathing change. Henry brought a pillow down. He slid it under Richard's head in place of his arm. Slowly, carefully, Henry slipped out from under Richard and off the bed. He found the armchair and sat down. Richard didn't wake completely but turned over on his side to resettle himself. His angelic cheek pressed against the pillow. Henry could watch this all day.

The door peeked out into the room softly. Henry looked up and saw Elizabeth with Duncan behind her. Henry put his finger to his mouth. He stood. Henry went to the door. They let him out into the hallway. He came out, mostly closing the door, leaving it ajar just enough to keep an eye on the sleeping child.

"He's worn out," Henry informed them.

"Why didn't you come back and join us?" Duncan replied.

"I don't want him to wake up alone." Henry looked through the crack in the door toward Richard.

"You're hovering," Duncan accused.

"He needs to know someone cares about him," Henry argued.

"He also needs to learn how to deal with fear on his own," Duncan asserted.

"He's not even five yet," Elizabeth protested.

"And impressionable," Duncan pointed out.

"Another reason not to have him around Arthur," Elizabeth insisted.

Duncan laughed. "You can crow about his failings all you want, but you have your own faults."

Henry rolled his eyes. He knew exactly where this was leading.

"What are you teaching Ricky when he sees a guy you're not married to coming out of your room after spending the night?" Duncan charged.

"That there is safety in numbers," Henry retorted. "Considering he has been so terrified he feels the need to sleep between us."

Duncan looked to his daughter for confirmation.

Elizabeth backed Henry up. "It's the only way we've

gotten him to sleep."

"He slept in his own room at the penthouse." Henry brushed the corner of his jaw with the back of his finger.

"Just let it go already. Returning to the penthouse isn't happening," Duncan ordered. "Be grateful I'm letting the two of you take him out to Liz's shoot tomorrow."

"So soon?" Henry questioned. He figured they'd have to wait until the month was out.

"Think of it as a test." Duncan stared down Henry coldly, just long enough for the other man to notice. Henry didn't flinch. Without waiting for a verbal response, Duncan continued. "I'm sure Richard will have fun. Maybe Tristian will take a couple headshots for him."

Henry frowned. "Richard doesn't need headshots." He crossed his arms over his chest.

"Richard should have his own modeling contract," Duncan pronounced.

"He's too young." Henry shook his head. "Let him be a kid."

Duncan beamed. "My grandson is adorable. It would be a shame not to show him off."

"I'm all for showing Richard off—just not putting him to work," Henry countered.

Duncan excused himself. "I've got to go make a few calls. Talk to you later, Lizzie."

Henry watched Duncan's retreating form. Once Duncan started down the stairs, Henry turned his eyes to Elizabeth. "I don't mind if he takes pictures on shoots with you, but ..."

"He's already done some solo shoots," she interjected. Henry raised an eyebrow. "I'm always there during them," Elizabeth assured him.

"That's not the issue," he countered.

"I was reluctant at first, but things happened," she replied.

"And just because I wasn't there then, I don't get a vote now?" Henry put his hands on his hips.

"I am not saying that." Elizabeth lifted her hand almost in a signal for him to calm down. Henry took a couple of deep breaths. "I just meant the cat is kind of out of the bag—not that he'll model again," she explained.

"Not on his own for a while," Henry asserted.

"Richard is comfortable during photoshoots. He sees it as completely normal." She forced a smiled. "It's Mama's job."

"It's not that it's a bad job, but he's too young to work. If he were older, I wouldn't have any problem with it—"

His words were cut off by a scream from the bed in the next room. Both parents ran to their son's side. Richard shot straight up in the bed.

"Ricky? We're right here," Henry soothed.

"It's OK, angel," Elizabeth cooed.

Richard held out his arms. Elizabeth accepted his hug. Henry rubbed Richard's back. Richard let go of Elizabeth and turned around to embrace Henry. Henry soaked in the contact.

"Are you all right?" Henry asked.

"I guess so," Richard replied. Henry brought Richard onto his lap.

"Do you think you can eat something after your nap?" Elizabeth asked.

Richard shook his head.

"How about we go outside and I'll teach you how to play catch? Or are you still too sleepy?" Henry suggested.

"I wanna play," Richard answered.

Henry bounced Richard on his knee. "All right." Henry

smiled. "Let's go find a ball." Henry set him on the floor. Richard tugged Henry up by the hand.

"Are you coming, Mama?" Richard requested.

"Of course I am!" Elizabeth affirmed cheerfully. She stood. "In fact, I think I know where a ball you can use is," Elizabeth added. She ducked into Richard's room and returned with a tennis ball. Elizabeth handed it to Henry. "I hope this will do."

"Not quite a baseball, but it works." Henry tossed the ball in the air to catch it in his palm.

He led his family down out of their wing through the living room, out to the backyard, past the patio, and into the large grassy area. "I'm going to toss the ball, and you catch it; then you toss it back to me, OK?" Henry explained. Richard nodded his understanding.

"It'll take some practice, so don't feel bad if you don't catch the ball immediately," Henry cautioned. Elizabeth hung back and watched.

Henry stepped a few feet away from Richard. "Here it comes," he called before Richard tried to catch it, but the ball slipped through his grasp. It fell by his feet.

"That's OK," Henry encouraged. "Pick it up and toss it to me." Richard did as he'd been directed. Henry caught it. "Ready to try again?"

This time Richard used both his hands to catch the ball. He held it up in the air. "Nice catch!" Henry cheered. "Now throw it back to me," Henry instructed. He held his hands open as Richard tossed the ball. Richard hauled back his arm and threw the ball with all his might. Henry moved his hand forward just slightly, catching the ball with ease. "You've got a great arm." Henry grinned. He tossed it back to Richard and the boy caught it again.

"All right!" Elizabeth praised.

This second time, it sailed by Henry. Hitting the ground, it got caught in a slope. The ball rolled along the grass until it stopped. "It's OK. I'll get it," Henry said. He ran in the direction the ball headed. Henry bent over to pick it up. As he straightened, he came face to face with little Tom. So much for a break from the other family. Henry continued to his full height, not sure of how to deal with the child.

Tom looked at him expectantly.

Silvia appeared at the back door of the mansion. "Why don't you go play with your mom?" Henry suggested. He caught Silvia's eyes and pointed to Tom. She called to her son and motioned for him to come back.

Once Henry was assured that Tom was attended to, he returned to where his family stood. He led Richard by the hand around the corner to the back of the pool house. Honestly, the less contact the two boys had with each other, the better, as far as Henry was concerned.

"You not playing with Tommy?" Richard said in a tone of awe. Most people, especially the man he called Daddy, would rather play with Tommy and ignore him. Not that "Daddy" played with either boy much.

"I know it's not nice to not include him, but remember we said you weren't going to play with him for a while. Besides, to tell you the truth, I'd kind of rather play with my little man." Henry ruffled Richard's sandy locks.

Chapter Eleven

E lizabeth grinned. "Hello, good looking."

"Did I pick the right shirt?" Henry ran his hand over the buttons.

Elizabeth approved. "White is perfect." It would look great in the photographs she hoped Tristian would take for her.

In a white polo shirt, Richard continued to play with Lucy where he sat at the end of the bed. "Hey, we kind of match." Henry tickled Richard's stomach. The boy laughed.

"It's time to go, angel," Elizabeth said. Richard sat Lucy on the bed and took his mother's hand.

Henry picked up a backpack of toys and distractions for Richard. He put his arm through the strap and slung it over his shoulder. "OK, let's get to the garage before anybody comes down for breakfast," Henry urged.

"We'll have to stop at the kitchen for our food." Elizabeth steered them in the right direction when they hit the bottom of the stairs.

"Aren't we going to pick up something on the way to the

studio?" Henry frowned.

"I already asked the cook for some berry smoothies," Elizabeth reported.

"Yummy," Richard interjected.

"I thought you'd like that," she replied.

They rounded the last corner before the kitchen to find Duncan leaning on the kitchen doorframe. "No time for breakfast?" he lifted a carton containing the aforementioned smoothies in to-go cups.

Elizabeth blinked rapidly. "Dad, you're up."

"Did you think you'd get to go out without saying good morning?" Duncan handed her the carryout carton.

"I'm just trying to get to the studio on time," she covered.

"Walk you to your car?" Duncan offered.

"OK," Elizabeth agreed. They walked in silence. Elizabeth tried to keep the pace as brisk as possible without having Richard fall behind.

When they got there, Duncan opened the door for them. "After you."

A driver stood by a town car. He opened the door as they entered.

"You can't be serious," Henry groaned.

Duncan smiled. "Albert will drive you today."

"A town car isn't necessary," Elizabeth protested. "We have our own vehicle."

"I'm afraid I must insist," Duncan said. He held out a debit card to Henry.

"What is this?" the younger man inquired.

"I've pulled some strings at your bank and straightened out your account for you," Duncan said.

Henry bit his bottom lip and raised an eyebrow.

"It's already activated." Duncan offered it out further.

"You shouldn't have." Henry reluctantly took the card. It was from the bank he used to use. The card had his name embossed on it.

Duncan smirked. "Nonsense."

"We better be heading out," Elizabeth urged.

"Be back before bedtime," Duncan reminded them. He leaned in to Elizabeth's ear. "Don't even think of running," he whispered. Duncan bent over and kissed the crown of Richard's head. "Have a great day, Ricky." He urged the boy toward the car. "Be on your best behavior," Duncan warned.

Richard was bouncing as they buckled him in his booster seat. "Are you excited, angel?" Elizabeth grinned. She gave him his smoothie.

Richard happily began to suck it down. His stomach still hurt a little, but he liked berries too much to pass them up.

Henry pushed the button that closed the partition for a bit of privacy. He waited until it was fully up before speaking.

"A second car pulled out after us," Henry notified her.

"I figured he'd have us followed," she sighed.

"Doesn't he have better things to do? This is ridiculous. He's already got a spy in the front," he muttered. Henry threw his head back and closed his eyes. Elizabeth stroked his arm. Henry shifted to settle into the seat.

———

Arthur slipped into the limo where Duncan waited.

"We're going to be late." Duncan took a sip from his coffee travel thermos.

Arthur shrugged. "You don't look too upset about that." There was a slight upward curve to the corner of his mentor's lips.

"Just see that you are on time tonight, or I will leave without you," Duncan asserted.

Arthur nodded his head. "Understood."

"If you can stay on track today, maybe you'll stop getting your butt handed to you by Oliver's wife," Duncan challenged. "I am planning to be home before my grandson gets there."

Arthur loosened his tie. "Why did you let them take Richard out anyway? You didn't even talk to me about it."

"I am doing this for you," Duncan asserted. "Someone has to stir some trouble up between those two and keep them from closing ranks."

"And what kind of trouble are you attempting to stir?" Arthur inquired.

"The photographer: I doubt she's told him about Tristian yet." Duncan smirked.

"Tristian? He was two years ago." Arthur frowned.

"To you maybe," Duncan said. "It's news to Henry."

"And he'll care because?" Arthur questioned.

"It's emotional and Henry puts more stock in emotions than you or I do," Duncan replied.

"You have a point there," Arthur agreed.

"You know if Tristian had asked, she would have left you for him." Duncan raised an eyebrow.

"He was never going to ask," Arthur scoffed. "Besides she's wanted to leave off and on. It was nothing special about him."

"No, that's on you." Duncan straightened his suit lapels.

RESTORATION

"What do you want for your birthday?"

Richard shrugged. Henry pressed his lips together. That was not an answer to his question.

Elizabeth snuggled in as close as the seatbelt would let her. "He'd love a ball and glove you know," she whispered to him.

Henry inhaled. "It's not enough."

"You don't have to give him anything extravagant." She laid her head on his shoulder. "I think having you around is the best present he could get."

He sighed. "It's my job to be there for him, not a gift."

"We'll figure something out," Elizabeth assured him.

"How much has changed since I've been to your photoshoots?" Henry asked.

"Not all that much. I have worked with most of this crew a lot before," Elizabeth answered.

"You and Duncan have mentioned the photographer by first name," Henry noted.

"Tristian is a good friend." She licked her lips. He nodded and took a sip of the smoothie through the straw.

The driver stopped in front of the studio. He got out and opened the door. "I'll be in the parking lot whenever you need me." Henry got out while Elizabeth unbuckled Richard. He helped the other two exit the vehicle. As they walked toward the glass front door, a roguish-looking fellow opened it. "Hiya, Lizbits!" the blond and blue-eyed photographer called out.

"Back at ya, Tris!" Elizabeth hollered back.

Tristian let all three of them enter before squatting down to Richard's height.

"Ricky, my little dude!" Tristian greeted with a warm smile. He squatted down and held up his hand. Richard gave him a high five.

"Who is this, dude?" Tristian motioned with his thumb toward Richard's older doppelganger.

"This is Henry." Elizabeth patted Henry's chest.

"The *Henry*?" Tristian pushed off of his knees to stand. She nodded. The photographer reached out his hand. "I'm Tristian. It's nice to finally meet you, Henry."

"Likewise," Henry replied. The two shook hands. Henry felt the photographer giving him a special once-over. If you squinted in just the right way, Henry kind of looked like him.

"The lights are getting set up, so we need you in hair and makeup, Liz," Tristian began.

"Hi, Louisa." Elizabeth waved as they entered the designated area.

"Have a seat," the makeup artist offered. Elizabeth sat in the chair in front of Louisa.

Richard got up on an unoccupied chair next to Elizabeth's and started to spin in it. Louisa laughed, "He is just too cute, Liz."

Henry stood close by the chair, making sure Richard didn't fall.

"So what are you torturing me with today?" Elizabeth deadpanned.

Tristian fluffed out her dark-brown, nearly black, hair. "We're going for early morning goddess," he said. Tristian turned to Louisa. "Natural, glowy, with a glamorous edge," he instructed.

"Oh, so you mean she doesn't need me?" Louisa deadpanned. "Fine, I can go home."

Elizabeth grabbed her hand, playing along. "You're staying here, sister. Someone needs to fix these raccoon eyes."

Louisa played along. "Pffft, you call those raccoon eyes? Honey, you should have seen the ones on the pop star I took care of for her music video yesterday."

Elizabeth turned to give the makeup artist better access to her face. "Work your magic."

Louisa worked quickly, getting the base of foundation and concealer applied first. "Close your eyes," she directed. Elizabeth complied. Louisa applied neutral eyeshadow with a small padded brush. Next came the mascara. Louisa finished the look with red lipstick. "All done!" she pronounced.

"What do you think, baby boy?" Elizabeth turned to Richard.

"You're pretty, Mama!" Richard proclaimed.

"Mama is very pretty," Henry agreed.

"Off to wardrobe with you!" Louisa directed.

Racks of clothes were lined up in the next room.

The stylist chose a denim button-up shirt dress and a black belt for the first outfit. "Come with me."

"I'll be right out. Listen to Henry, OK?" Elizabeth directed. Richard nodded.

The two women disappeared behind a couple of privacy curtains. "Wow, two minutes. It's like you're a pro or something," Tristian quipped.

Elizabeth gave it right back. "Considering I've been doing this since I was seven, I'd say so."

Tristian looked to their companions. "Can I borrow her for a minute?" Henry nodded. Tristian drew her aside.

"Are you OK?" Tristian inquired.

"Fine," she assured him.

"Oliver told me Duncan had you dragged back to the estate," Tristian informed her.

"It was Richard he dragged back, but that's mere semantics," Elizabeth replied.

He frowned. "Same difference—where Ricky goes you go."

"At least Henry is with us. He makes it somehow bearable." She smiled softly, angling back to see Henry making silly faces to get a laugh out of their boy.

"Can I ask you for a favor?" Elizabeth asked.

"Sure thing," Tristian agreed.

"I was hoping maybe you could sneak in a few pictures of the three of us?" Elizabeth requested.

"Anything for you, doll." Tristian winked at her.

They rejoined Henry and Richard. The foursome continued into the studio.

Elizabeth walked on to check out the set.

"How about some music?" Tristian offered.

"Set the tone, maestro." Elizabeth waved her hand.

Tristian took up a remote and hit play on it. He held up his camera and looked through the viewfinder. Tristian brought it back down with a frown. He motioned his head toward a lamp. "Can we reangle that light down about ten degrees?" Tristian directed.

The tech closest to the lamp adjusted it.

Elizabeth worked her angles, interacting with the set.

"All right, Lizbits, eyes on me." Tristian moved in for some close-ups. Elizabeth flicked her eyes up and looked at him over her shoulder. They took several more pics. "OK, got it." Tristian brought the camera down. "Next outfit."

Elizabeth took off the high heels and carried them in one

hand. She sauntered over to Henry and Richard.

"Really, Liz?" Tristian teased. "In the middle of a shoot?"

"It's just lipstick." Elizabeth waved him off.

"Kiss me too, Mama!" Richard insisted. Elizabeth leaned down and kissed his forehead.

The stylist motioned for her to come back and get changed. "I'll be right back, baby," Elizabeth told Richard.

Henry stood dazed, watching Elizabeth head back to hair and makeup.

Tristian snickered. "You're going to want to wipe that off."

Henry's fingers slowly drifted up to his lips, now tinted by a transfer of Elizabeth's red lipstick. He began to rub the substance away with his thumb.

Tristian retrieved a wet wipe out of the pack on the cleaning supply table. "Here," he offered it to Henry.

Henry chuckled. "Thanks." He cleaned off his thumb. Then wiped off the residue from his mouth.

Tristian lifted his camera to check on the frames of film left.

"A Canon EOS," Henry noted. "Nice."

"You know your cameras," Tristian remarked.

"I double majored in studio art and photography." Henry shrugged. "I had a Canon, but it wasn't anywhere near that level."

"This one is getting to be an old bird, but she's the best," Tristian replied. "Have you tried any of those new digital cameras?"

Henry shook his head. "They're coming out with that kind of stuff?" Tristian nodded. "Think you'll ever switch over?" Henry inquired.

"When the quality gets there, possibly," Tristian replied.

Elizabeth walked back out in a white, flowy lace dress. She returned to her place on the set.

"Wanna give it a go?" Tristian offered.

"You mean it?" Henry queried.

Tristian laughed. "It's insured." He handed the camera over.

Henry lay down on the floor, angling the camera up. "Hey, babe," he called to get Elizabeth's attention. She flicked sultry eyes to him. He took several pictures before twisting to change the angle.

"Hey, Ricky, why don't you get out there with Mama?" Henry looked back to his son and flicked his head toward Elizabeth. Richard clapped and ran over to Elizabeth. You didn't have to ask him twice.

Henry snapped away as she spun their son around. Their noses and foreheads touching. Henry beamed at what he saw through the viewfinder.

Tristian nudged her. "Your turn. Get in there!"

Henry handed the camera back to him.

He didn't even notice the camera going off as Tristian snapped away.

———

"Are you hungry?" Henry asked.

"Not really." Richard looked over to the curtains behind which his mother was changing again.

She appeared back in her street clothes.

"Do we really need to come back for round two? You and Tristian got through like twenty outfits," Henry questioned.

"We get things done fast because I've learned what he wants for a shot," Elizabeth said. "Which means we get a lot of work done."

"So the two of you got to know each other well?" he inquired.

"Is somebody jealous?" Elizabeth quipped.

"Maybe a touch," Henry admitted jokingly, motioned with his fingers. A pit formed in Elizabeth's stomach.

"Louisa, could you?" Elizabeth pointed to Richard.

"Come on, honey," Louisa beckoned. She led him out to give his parents some privacy.

Henry chuckled. "I was teasing."

"I haven't told you everything." Elizabeth wrung her hands.

He took her hands in his. "You don't have to."

She blew out a breath. "Tristian is an almost," Elizabeth explained, almost afraid to look at Henry.

He smiled. "Lucky bastard," Henry teased in a warm tone.

"A couple of years ago. It was just a really, really bad time, and he helped Richard and me hide out for a few weeks," she went on.

"Good for him," he said.

"You don't have to pretend like you're OK with it," she said.

"I'm not pretending." Henry caught her eyes. Elizabeth held her breath. "I can't judge what you did or didn't do to stay sane." He added, "I love you." Henry leaned in and brushed his lips over hers. What he intended to be a tender, short kiss quickly heated up. Elizabeth brought his hands to the side of her waist. Henry backed her up until they hit into the makeup counter. His hands drifted up her ribs.

They heard the click of high heels and quickly broke apart. A dark-haired woman froze in the doorway. "Sorry, I didn't mean to interrupt," Kate apologized.

"It's OK. We were getting a little carried away." Henry pulled her into his arms.

"Babe, this is Tristian's fiancé, Katrina Rios." Elizabeth began introductions.

Kate tipped her head. "Hello."

"Kate, this is Henry Angevin." Elizabeth patted his chest.

"Nice to meet you." He reached out and shook her hand.

"Kate, you back there?" Tristian called.

"Coming," Kate called.

The three headed out into the hallway. Richard ran over to his mother. "Thanks, Louisa," Elizabeth said. The makeup artist gave a brief wave and then left.

"There you are," Tristian crooned to Kate.

"Ready to eat, honey?" Kate joined him.

"Yeah, they don't need me for the switch over." Tristian nodded.

Kate looked over to the little family. "We're heading out to lunch. You guys want to come with?"

"We've got an almost five-year-old with us." Elizabeth wrapped an arm around Richard and tucked him closer to her. He held onto the hem of her shirt.

"He's fine." Kate smiled at the boy. Richard batted his eyelashes at her. "Oh, you are going to be quite the heartbreaker when you grow up," Kate gushed.

Kate leaned forward over the table. "How did the two of you meet?"

"A mutual friend of ours invited me to one of Henry's showings," Elizabeth answered.

"Showings?" Kate questioned.

"Henry is a painter," Elizabeth explained.

"That is seriously cool." Kate tipped her head toward Henry.

"I don't paint so much anymore." Henry took up his glass of water.

Elizabeth smirked. "I tripped and he caught me, so I guess you could kind of say it was lust at first fall."

"I could tell from the pretty heavy petting I walked in on," Kate teased, careful in her choice of words because of the youngster sitting at the end of the table.

"Well, that wasn't completely his doing. I kind of egged him on." Elizabeth bit her bottom lip and raised an eyebrow saucily.

Kate giggled.

Tristian slid back into his seat. "What did I miss?"

Kate rubbed his shoulder. "Nothing." They all began to dig into their meals. "Did you know Henry is a painter?" she asked.

"Yeah, Liz might have mentioned it a time or two." Tristian smiled at the other couple.

Their server brought out the food they'd ordered. She set a bowl of macaroni and cheese in front of Richard.

"It's hot, angel," Elizabeth warned. She looked up from her son to see a woman staring at them from across the room. She had twenty years on them. Her hair was nearly the shade of Henry's, sandy blond.

"Do you see who I see?" Henry cut his steak, trying to look normal.

Elizabeth nodded. She discreetly wrote something down on a napkin. She slid the napkin over the table to Henry. "Can you get this to her?" she requested.

"Sure." Henry slipped it into his pocket. Leaning over the table, he kissed Elizabeth. Henry excused himself. "I'll be back in a flash."

Puzzled, Kate looked to Tristian for an explanation. "Let's just say life is complicated right now," Elizabeth said.

Seeing Henry leave the table, the older woman excused herself from her companions. They met in a mostly shielded area in front of the restrooms.

"Henry," she said.

"In the flesh." He kissed both of her cheeks. "Hello, Victoria."

"It's good to see you again," she answered.

"You look well." Henry smiled.

"I'd be better if I could talk to Liz," Victoria replied. "Since she sent you instead of coming to my table, I assume Duncan put his foot back down."

He checked around to make sure no prying eyes were on them. Henry slipped the napkin into Victoria's hand. "From Elizabeth," he relayed in a quiet tone.

"Thank you." Victoria carefully tucked it into her clutch.

"A meeting location?" she inquired.

"Don't know." Henry shrugged.

"You didn't read it—good man." Victoria nodded her head in approval.

"Some things are private," he replied.

"Privacy is a very elusive luxury these days." She stuck

her clutch tightly under her arm.

"Tell me about it," Henry muttered.

"I suppose Duncan has you all back at the mansion again," Victoria deduced. Henry didn't say anything, but he nodded. "Does this mean you and Liz are back together?" she asked.

"You could say that, but technically we never broke up," Henry said.

Victoria cast her eyes to the ground momentarily before locking eyes with him. She frowned. "You better do right by Liz; not many people do."

"She's been through hell," Henry acknowledged.

"Losing you back then, it nearly destroyed my daughter," Victoria relayed.

"I am going to spend the rest of my life making it up to her," Henry vowed.

"Good." Victoria pressed her lips together. "I guess we both better be getting back to our tables."

"Hope we see you again soon," he replied.

Henry turned to return to Elizabeth. Victoria caught him by his bicep as he was leaving. He turned back to her. "Tell Liz and Ricky I love them," she requested.

"I will," Henry promised.

Chapter Twelve

"What is the purpose of this excursion?" the guard eyed the driver and her companion in the passenger seat.

"We need to do some birthday shopping," Elizabeth said.

"Just a moment," the guard said. He stepped inside to make a call. Elizabeth drummed her fingernails on the steering wheel. She kept herself from glancing toward the back seat.

The guard returned. "All right, you're cleared." He pushed a button. The gate lifted.

"Thanks." Henry tipped his head.

Once through the gate, the parents breathed a sigh of relief. They drove a good distance away before finding a safe place to pull over.

"You can come out, angel," Elizabeth beckoned.

Richard peeked his head out from under the blanket he'd hid under. "You can get in your booster," Elizabeth directed. He pushed the blanket aside and climbed over into his safety seat.

Henry unbuckled and got out of the car. He went back to Richard. Henry opened the door. He connected Richard's buckles. They clicked in. "There you go," Henry said. Henry returned to his seat. Elizabeth pulled them out back onto the road.

"You OK, angel?" Elizabeth checked for him in the rearview mirror.

"Yes, Mama." Richard nodded.

They continued on their way to the mall. Elizabeth parked them in the section closest to the food court. Richard kicked his feet playfully as he waited for her to come around and get him. "Hey." She smiled as she opened his door. Elizabeth helped Richard out of his seat and set him on his feet beside the vehicle. He stayed in place while Elizabeth locked and then closed his door. She took him by the hand. "Let's go."

They met Henry behind the car. Henry's heart skipped a beat as Richard's little fingers reached out for his hand. Richard bounced along between his parents.

Elizabeth scanned the teeming room. Her eyes landed on Victoria as the older woman stood from her table and waved at them.

"Nonna!" Richard called. He let go of his parents' hands. Richard raced to Victoria with his arms wide open.

"There's my little man." Victoria hugged him tightly. Richard squeezed her back. "How is Lucy?" she inquired.

"Good, she's napping in the car," he answered. He'd brought her with him so Tommy wouldn't get ahold of her. Richard stepped back and let Elizabeth have her turn.

"Hello, darling." Victoria reached out for her daughter.

Elizabeth embraced her. "I'm sorry it took so long to meet. Work has been crazy."

"And your father's been crazy too," Victoria finished. "I know what it's like when Duncan's throwing one of his power trips."

"He isn't even trying to dial it back," Elizabeth remarked.

Victoria brushed a stray blond hair back behind her ear. While Elizabeth got her dark hair and facial features from Duncan, her eyes and her figure she inherited from her mother.

"We're not at the penthouse anymore, but you probably already figured that out," Elizabeth informed her.

"When you didn't show up for our first scheduled lunch and I couldn't reach you I knew," Victoria concurred. "It's been two weeks."

"Feels like two months," Henry muttered.

"Hello, Henry." Victoria hugged him as well.

"Hi, Victoria," he greeted with a warm smile.

"Would anyone like to get a little something to eat?" Victoria offered. "There's a soft pretzel shop in the corner."

Elizabeth accepted. "I'm sure Ricky would love one."

"I know how you enjoy them too. You're young. You can handle the carbs," Victoria said.

"I'm t'irsty," Richard said.

"Nonna will get you a lemonade too." Victoria patted his hand.

She took up her soda and led the troupe over to the pretzel shop. They gave their order and then stepped to the side to wait.

"I've been dying to check in with you, but I figured if I called the mansion it would just make things worse." Victoria frowned.

Elizabeth blew out a breath. She hated that it was the truth.

They picked up their order and began to walk around the mall as they ate.

RESTORATION

"What story did you tell Duncan to let you out?" Victoria inquired.

"Actually, we have Richard's tutor covering for us. Dad doesn't know we brought him out," Henry explained.

"You're risking an awful lot to come see me," Victoria noted.

"It's worth it," Elizabeth pronounced. Her son deserved a relationship with his only living grandmother.

They came upon a sports store as they finished their pretzels.

"Will you ladies be OK distracting Ricky while I check out a store?" Henry requested.

"Birthday," Elizabeth mouthed to her mother while pointing to Richard.

"Of course," Victoria agreed.

"You're going?" Richard questioned.

Henry knelt down to Richard's level. "I just want to pick up some birthday surprises for you, OK?" he promised. Henry caught Richard's worried eyes. "I'll meet up with you …" He trailed off looking at Elizabeth.

"At the Sunset Music store," she finished.

"At the Sunset Music store in twenty minutes," Henry added.

"OK." Richard frowned sadly.

"Hey, I love you, little prince." Henry kissed the temple of Richard's head as he stood.

Richard clutched his mother's hand as they walked on. He turned back for a moment to see Henry slip inside a store.

"How are things with you and Henry?" Victoria inquired.

"Good, we're good. I mean, given the circumstances," Elizabeth said.

"Any problems?" Victoria questioned with genuine concern.

"He's bottling a lot more up than he used to," Elizabeth admitted.

Richard paused when he came to a store that had a canvas and easel in the window display. He looked up at the sign over the door.

"We go in t'is store, Mama?" Richard requested.

"You want to get something for Henry?" Elizabeth asked.

Richard nodded his head.

"All right," Elizabeth agreed. They stepped inside the shop and surveyed the layout of the store.

"OK, what are we looking for?" Victoria questioned.

"Brushes," Richard stated.

"Why paintbrushes?" Elizabeth asked.

"Ri's brushes aren't so nice. Maybe better brushes 'elp 'im paint again," Richard reasoned.

"Oh, you are so sweet." Victoria squeezed him tight to her side.

Elizabeth led them to the proper aisle. "These are for oil paint, the kind Henry uses." She pointed out a large section of brushes. Richard went off to pick from them.

"So Henry's having trouble painting?" Victoria whispered.

"You could say that. He hasn't been painting at all," Elizabeth answered. "Maybe we're all pushing too hard. He's only been out two-and-a-half weeks."

"Out?" Victoria's brow furrowed.

"He was stuffed in a so-called mental institution the whole time," Elizabeth answered. She selected a few brushes from the upper shelves where Richard couldn't reach.

"All five years? I can't imagine what he must have gone through," Victoria replied.

"Arthur and Dad basically buried him there," Elizabeth added.

Victoria frowned. "Are you sure your father was involved?"

"You don't think so?" Elizabeth tilted her head.

"I'll admit Duncan plays dirty," Victoria began. The two women here knew that better than anyone.

"He won't deny participating." Elizabeth fingered another brush.

"I'm sorry." Victoria frowned.

"Can't say I'm surprised," Elizabeth replied.

"He is used to getting his way." Victoria looked after Richard as he sorted through the aisle.

"Don't feel bad that you like to see the best in people," Elizabeth said.

"One of my biggest weaknesses," Victoria admitted, "especially with Duncan. Narcissists can be very charming when they want something."

"How'd you end up marrying Dad anyway?" Elizabeth questioned.

"I loved him once upon a time. I did. You came from love. Never doubt that," Victoria encouraged.

"I know you loved him, Mom, but I'm not so sure he returned the feeling." Elizabeth stared down at the brush she had just picked up. She drew her finger over the soft bristles.

"I believe he loved me at one point, but he loves the idea of a son more, and I got too old to give him one." Victoria shrugged.

"You tried, Mom." Elizabeth rubbed Victoria's arm.

Richard brought over the bundle he had collected. To Elizabeth's surprise, they all had matching handles.

He pulled out the wallet he kept the allowance Elizabeth gave him from his modeling jobs in; the rest was put in an account for him. Richard got out two bills. "Is t'is enou'?" he held them up to her.

"Oh, angel, that is more than enough," Elizabeth said. "But I was going to help you buy them."

"No, my gift for Ri," Richard protested.

"You are as stubborn as Henry is," Elizabeth quipped.

Richard grinned mischievously. He wasn't sure what stubborn meant, but Mama really liked Henry so being compared to him had to be a good thing.

***

"Do you carry kids' jerseys?" Henry asked.

"Depends on the team," the employee said in an unspoken question.

"Dodgers," Henry said.

"We always keep those in stock," the employee replied. "There are caps as well."

"Awesome, I'll definitely take one of those too," Henry replied.

"The kids' section is beside the women's section on your right," the cashier indicated.

"Thanks." Henry tipped his head.

He headed over. Henry found the jerseys. He went for the correct team and sorted through the racks to find a size small for Richard. The baseball caps lined the wall.

RESTORATION

Henry picked out an appropriate one.

Out of the corner of his eye, he spotted some children's bats on the adjacent wall. Henry set the jersey and cap aside. There was a T-ball set next to them. He picked a kit up and had a look. That would be perfect. Now the only thing missing was a glove for Richard. Henry searched through the children's section. With none to be found there, he headed for the regular gloves. The gloves at end of the aisle where large so he went all the way down to the end. "Bingo." He smirked coming to the right size. He chose a black glove with red lacing for Richard.

Henry brought his load up front and got in line. Once it was his turn, he sat the trove down on the counter.

"Wow, that is one lucky kid," the cashier muttered.

"He's a special boy," Henry said.

The cashier rang up the items, "That'll be $70.43."

Henry handed him his debit card, knowing Duncan was probably tracing the account. Once it cleared, the cashier gave him a receipt to sign, which Henry did.

Henry took his bags and made a beeline for the music store. He met up with the group he was looking for as they came to the door themselves.

"Hiya, little prince," Henry greeted.

"Ri," Richard returned.

"See, I told you I'd be back," Henry said. Richard smiled up at him.

They spent the next hour visiting and losing track of time. When they had to leave, Victoria walked them out to the car.

Elizabeth lifted Richard into his booster seat and buckled him in. Elizabeth stepped out so Victoria could say goodbye to Richard.

"See you in a little over a week." Victoria leaned in and kissed Richard's cheek.

"Bye, Nonna." Richard returned the kiss.

She pulled herself out and Elizabeth closed the door.

"Bye, Mom." Elizabeth's voice cracked.

"This isn't goodbye forever." Victoria licked her lips. "I'm coming for Richard's birthday."

"I can't say those plans still stand," Elizabeth warned.

"Whatever is planned I'll be there," Victoria vowed. "I'm not going to miss it."

"If I can't contact you, I'll have Oliver let you know what's going on," Elizabeth promised.

Elizabeth blinked away tears as she tugged the driver's side door open.

Victoria stood in the spot waving until the car exited the parking lot. Richard waved at his grandmother until he couldn't see her anymore.

"Remember: this is our secret," Elizabeth instructed. "We can't tell anyone we visited Nonna."

Richard hung his head in understanding. "Granddad would get mad."

———

"Ms. Harper?"

"Yes, Felix." Elizabeth leaned back from her spot on the couch.

"A Mr. Grammar is here to see you. He just got through the gate," the butler relayed.

"Thank you. I'll meet him in the entryway," she said.

Felix nodded and went to answer the door.

"I'll be right back," Elizabeth said.

"Ok, Mama," Richard acknowledged but kept his eyes on the TV.

"You can bring Tristian back here if he wants to hang out for a bit," Henry offered.

"We'll see." She kissed his cheek as she straightened her legs and pushed herself up onto her feet.

Leaving the room, Elizabeth began to navigate to the front of the mansion. She got to the entryway as Felix opened the door for Tristian.

"Hey, Lizbits," Tristian greeted as he walked through the door.

Elizabeth smiled. "Hi."

"I brought the pictures you asked for." Tristian lifted a large cardboard envelope along with a manila envelope behind it.

"Oh, you didn't have to go through all that trouble," she replied. "A messenger would have worked just as well."

He smirked. "Yeah, but then I'd miss that pretty face of yours."

"Flatterer," Elizabeth snorted.

"I call it like I see it." Tristian threw his hands up.

"Well, thank you for bringing the photos all this way," she said.

"Are Henry and Ricky around?" he inquired.

Elizabeth beamed. "My guys are in the den watching the game."

"Who's playing?" he inquired.

"Henry's favorite team: the Dodgers," she revealed.

Tristian play-hissed. "I'll try not to hold that against him," he quipped.

She snickered. "He's trying to get Richard into baseball."

"How's that going?" Tristian bit the inside of his cheek.

"Ricky's been enjoying it," Elizabeth replied. "Whether it's the game or the time he's getting to spend with Henry is anybody's guess."

"I'm glad to hear they seem to be bonding OK," he said.

"Richard is definitely warming up to Henry." She nodded.

"Speaking of which, I was actually hoping I could talk to Henry," Tristian said.

"Why don't we go join them in the den?" She motioned behind her.

"Lead the way," Tristian replied.

They walked shoulder to shoulder down the hall and through what Tristian assumed was the living room.

"A guy could easily get lost in this place." Tristian's eyes swept around, looking from corner to corner.

"The house doesn't have a complicated layout. It's just big," Elizabeth replied. "I don't think you've set foot in the mansion before."

Tristian nodded. "It's my first time here."

"I guess Dad scared you off." She shrugged.

"Duncan has that effect on people," he replied. Tristian waited a beat before changing the topic. "You and Kate kind of warmed up to each other the other day," he noted.

"Lunch was nice." She nodded her head.

"I hope it continues," Tristian added.

They found the father and son still watching the game.

"Hey, Tristian." Henry waved from his spot on the couch. Richard sat curled into Henry's side.

"What's the score?" Tristian inquired.

"Tied three to three," Henry reported.

"Sounds like a nail-biter," Tristian remarked. He handed over the packet to Henry. "You have a beautiful family, Henry," the photographer said.

Henry smiled. "Thank you."

It was now a commercial, so Henry opened the packet to look at the pictures.

"Why don't you take a seat?" Elizabeth motioned over to one of the armchairs as she returned to her spot beside Henry.

"These are great," Elizabeth said, watching Henry flip through them.

"I've got something to talk to you about," Tristian said.

"Shoot," Henry directed.

"They want to use your photo for the magazine cover," Tristian explained.

"Really?" Henry's eyes widened.

"Don't sound surprised. It was a great shot," Tristian rejoined.

"Is this OK with you?" Henry asked.

"They're still using mine in the spread." Tristian smiled.

"So what do I need to do?" Henry questioned.

"I've got the papers for you to sign: my usual contract, but you can have a lawyer look over it for you," Tristian said.

Henry picked up a pen from a notepad on the side table. "If Elizabeth trusts you, I trust you."

"You might want to get yourself an agent," Tristian advised. "And a new camera."

"Maybe I will." Henry signed in the appropriate spots.

"They sent me with a check for you." Tristian dug out a letter-size envelope from his jean's back pocket.

Henry accepted the envelope and opened it. "Is this

correct?" Henry questioned looking at the amount. It had a couple more zeros than he had been expecting. Tristian nodded. "Looks like we're eating pizza tonight!" Henry held up his hand. Richard gave him a high five.

"Got plans for dinner?" Henry inquired.

"I'm cooking for Kate," Tristian declined, "Raincheck?"

"Yeah, no prob. Maybe you can bring Kate along next time," Henry offered.

"That would be great." Tristian smiled.

"Before I go, Lizbits, I need to ask a favor," Tristian said. "I know I should be talking to your agent about this."

"You got another job for me?" she shifted.

"I really need you on this swimsuit shoot," Tristian began. "It's in two months."

"Where are you shooting?" Elizabeth inquired.

"Tahiti," he answered.

"I don't think Dad will let me on a plane with Richard," Elizabeth began. "And I can't leave him and Henry here."

"If it'll help, I'll talk to him," Tristian offered.

"Talk to who about what?" Duncan stepped into the room. Tristian stood.

"Dad, you're home early," Elizabeth said.

"I wanted to hear how your shopping trip went," Duncan replied.

"It was successful," Elizabeth said.

"Nice to see you again, Mr. Grammar." Duncan shook his hand. "What brings you out here?"

"I was hoping to convince Liz to come on a location photoshoot," Tristian answered.

"Where would that be taking place exactly?" Duncan looked between Tristian and Elizabeth.

Tristian made his pitch. "Tahiti. This is a big one. It's a step away from the swimsuit edition of *Sports Illustrated*, and if I get that through this, you know who I'm taking with me."

Duncan turned to Henry. "Are you OK with her doing swimsuit shoots?"

"As long as I get a copy of the magazine." Henry smirked.

"You know the exposure the swim cover of *Sports Illustrated* gets," Tristian contended.

"She has bigger things to be worried about right now," Duncan said. "I think it might be best if she focused on her marriage."

Elizabeth's shoulders tensed.

"I'll go and let you get back to watching your game." Tristian tipped his head. "If you all change your minds, you know where to find me."

"Felix will show you out," Duncan said.

"Thanks." Tristian slipped out the den door to the waiting butler. He couldn't get away from Duncan soon enough.

"I'm surprised to find you all in here. You three practically live in the pool house," Duncan said; a frown tugged at the corner of his lips.

"Baseball's on, Granddad." Richard pointed to the TV.

"How many innings to go?" Duncan asked. If his grandson liked it, he'd feign some type of interest.

Richard turned questioning eyes to Henry. "Six," Henry answered. "It's one of our guys coming up to bat."

Richard watched the screen breathlessly as the pitcher let the ball fly. The batter swung, knocking the ball out of the park, and then started running for the bases.

"'Ome run!" Richard clapped.

"Someone went on a splurge at the mall," Duncan noted.

"I'm not so sure I'm done birthday shopping yet." Henry grinned.

"Save some stuff for the rest of us," Elizabeth quipped. She trailed her fingertips up the back of his neck and played with the tips of his blond hair.

Duncan straightened his shoulders. "I need you to walk the red carpet for Spring Fire's opening."

"Dad, you know I hate those things," Elizabeth objected.

"It'll get you some of that exposure Tristian was just crowing about," Duncan countered.

"Huge difference between a high-profile shoot and a movie premiere." She raised an eyebrow.

"A little support for your old man would be nice," Duncan said. Henry tore his gaze from the television just long enough to give Duncan the side eye.

"Fine, I'll dress up and go to your opening," Elizabeth agreed, "On two conditions."

"What do you want?" Duncan rolled his eyes.

"Number one: we get to take Richard out for his birthday as planned," she asserted.

Duncan shrugged. "All right, I was going to allow that anyway."

"Number two: you make sure Arthur is not around on Richard's birthday," Elizabeth insisted.

"Oh, come on, Lizzie. Banning a father from his son's birthday—" Duncan began to protest.

She crossed her arms over her chest. "That one is nonnegotiable."

Chapter Thirteen

R ichard poked his head in from the patio doors. "Lucy?" He spotted his bear sitting across the room on the couch. Mama and Ri could still see him if he went inside. Richard couldn't hear anyone in there.

Richard didn't see Arthur crossing the room. "Hey! Watch where you're going, Stupid," Arthur barked.

"I ... I ... I'm s-s-sorry," Richard stuttered. He cowered, inching away.

Arthur looked down at the little boy. He saw red. Arthur hauled his arm over his shoulder. He struck Richard's cheek with the back of his hand. The force knocked Richard flat on his back. An involuntary yelp came from Richard as he fell.

"Get up," Arthur ordered.

Richard got to his elbows to comply when he heard Henry come in from the patio.

"Hey!" Henry called. He placed himself between Arthur and Richard.

"Mind your own business," Arthur shot back.

"Richard is my business," Henry declared.

Arthur clenched his fist. He took a swing at Henry. Henry, ready for the punch, grabbed Arthur's arm midair. With his free hand, he shoved Arthur's shoulder to spin him. Henry pinned his arm behind his back.

"Raise your hand to hit Richard again, and I'll break it," Henry hissed in his opponent's ear. He gave a slight shove as he let go of Arthur. Arthur tumbled over the couch and landed on the floor on the other side.

"Are you OK, little prince?" Henry questioned. Richard didn't respond. Henry turned around. Richard watched him wide-eyed from his place on the floor. Henry leaned over and offered Richard a hand up. Richard hesitantly put his little hand in Henry's larger one. Henry pulled him up to his feet.

He reached down and hooked a finger under Richard's chin. The boy tensed at the touch but allowed Henry to angle his face to see the cheek better. It had a large red mark across it. Richard saw Henry's face soften. The father squatted down to his son's level. Henry looked Richard in the eyes. "I'm sorry." Henry rubbed Richard's back. Richard relaxed into the hug.

"Wa-want Lu-Luc ..." Richard fought to get control of his tongue.

"Lucy?" Henry said the name for him. Richard nodded. "She in here?" Henry asked.

From separate directions, Duncan and Elizabeth entered as Arthur picked himself up off the floor.

"What happened in here?" Duncan probed. Neither of the older men spoke, so Duncan looked to his grandson.

"Daddy slapped me," Richard reported.

Elizabeth immediately knelt down and began to check over her son. He had a large red mark across his skin. She winced. "Oh, angel ..."

"I-I-I'm O-O-O-OK, Mama," Richard professed.

Elizabeth crushed her son to her. "No, it's not OK." She looked to her father, who was giving Arthur a withering glare.

"Another round of anger management sounds in order," Duncan warned.

"Oh, he needs more than that," Elizabeth asserted.

"How did Arthur end up on the floor?" Duncan questioned.

Henry arched his brow, pushing himself back to a standing position. No verbal response followed. Duncan already knew—no use in wasting his breath.

Arthur opened his mouth to explain.

"Go to work!" Elizabeth snapped.

"You might want to stay there," Henry charged.

If they'd had time, maybe Duncan would have let them continue, but today he didn't quite have that luxury. "I'll meet you in the limo," Duncan said. Arthur took that as a directive and made himself scarce.

"What do you have to say for yourself?" Duncan raised an eyebrow.

"Arthur's got no excuse abusing a kid," Henry charged. "If you won't step in, I will."

"Sometimes a parent needs to discipline their child." The older man tilted his head in challenge.

"That wasn't discipline!" Henry thundered.

The words barely left his mouth when the butler entered. "Ms. Wallace has arrived for Master Richard's session," Felix announced.

"See her in," Duncan directed.

The men continued to stare each other down. Jessica

surveyed the adults in the room and shivered. She went straight for her young charge with a smile.

"Are you ready, Richard?" Jessica held out her hand. Richard placed his hand in hers.

"Henry and I will be in our wing if you need anything," Elizabeth said.

"We'll find you when we're done." Jessica nodded.

"Can Mama come too?" Richard asked.

"It's all right," Elizabeth coaxed. "I'll be fine. Go with Ms. Jessica."

Richard trudged along beside his tutor. They waited for the pair to clear before resuming their argument.

"Richard didn't do anything wrong," Elizabeth asserted.

"He only went back in because he forgot Lucy. He loves that bear," Henry argued.

"I know," Duncan grumbled. "Vicki gave him that stupid thing for his second birthday, and he hasn't let go of it since."

"She helps him cope," Elizabeth said.

Duncan checked his watch. No matter how good his driver was with the traffic, they were going to be late. "Look, I've got an important meet and greet at the office this morning so let's just call this over," he suggested. Henry shook his head. Duncan turned his attention to his daughter. "Remember: Spring Fire's opening tonight."

"I'll be there. You better keep up your end of the deal," Elizabeth replied.

Duncan pressed his lips together. "Don't you trust me?" he questioned.

"No, I don't." She crossed her arms over her chest.

Duncan pressed his lips together. "I'll see you later." He headed for the garage.

Henry went over to the couch. He plucked up Lucy before sitting. Henry studied the bear for a moment. He laid his head against the top of the couch.

Elizabeth draped her arms over him from behind. "What's wrong?"

"I think I blew it," he sighed.

"I don't care what Dad says or thinks," she said.

"Not with your dad," Henry clarified.

"Then who?" Elizabeth asked.

He angled his chin up to angle his head. Henry locked eyes with her. "Richard's scared of me again."

"How do you figure that?" She frowned.

"I got into it with Arthur right in front of him," he pointed out.

"Honey, you intervened when he was being hurt. You had a good reason," Elizabeth insisted.

"His eyes when I checked on him …" Henry shut his own orbs.

"You forget that Arthur was still in the room. He instills a lot of fear in Richard," Elizabeth countered.

"He was looking at me," he argued.

"Richard knows you were protecting him." She rested her forehead on his arms. "He's still processing."

"All he saw was me getting angry." Henry mentally kicked himself.

"That's a very human reaction," Elizabeth asserted. "He's seen me fight with Arthur."

"You're his mother, he doesn't know who I am; I haven't earned his trust yet and with this display," he blew out a breath, "it's ten steps back."

"Richard just might surprise you." She got up.

Henry stared at the teddy bear in his hands. "I'll have to rein myself in better."

"Better? Bottling up your anger is a recipe for disaster," Elizabeth insisted.

"Do I have any better options?" he snapped. Henry hung his head. "I'm sorry."

"You can voice your frustrations to me." She rounded the couch to stand in front of him. Elizabeth craned down to catch his eyes. "I am not afraid of you," she added.

"Thanks for saying that."

"I do worry about you, though. I've seen you twitch in your sleep when you dream," she revealed.

"They're just dreams," he dismissed it.

"If you are afraid to talk with me about it, maybe hanging out with Oliver is in order," Elizabeth suggested.

"It's not his problem." Henry frowned.

"Beating yourself up is not going to help anything," Elizabeth admonished lovingly.

Henry kept his mouth shut and his eyes on Lucy.

Elizabeth decided to switch gears. "Listen, I have to go to that stupid opening tonight. At the moment I don't have Richard to distract me, so that has become your job."

"How exactly do you suggest I distract you?" he asked.

"I can think of a few things," she offered saucily.

Henry raised his head. "Oh?"

"Come on," Elizabeth beckoned. He got to his feet and took her hand. Together, they exited the living room and climbed the stairs to their wing, neither of them saying a word. They slipped into their room quietly. He set Richard's teddy bear in a chair.

Without a word, Elizabeth leaned back on the door to close

it.

Seeing her draped against the door nearly had Henry panting. He groaned appreciatively. "Tell me we are alone."

"Those who shall remain nameless have left for work," she said.

Not using their names drew a chuckle from Henry. He smirked. "Thank you for that."

"Richard is with Jessica for his session, so yeah, for now we are alone." Elizabeth pulled away from him. She turned the tab to lock the door and then stepped further into the room.

"Where are you going?" Henry asked as he followed her.

"I'm going to have a shower," she informed him. "Want to join me?"

"Are you sure, Elizabeth?" Henry inquired. She smiled as he swayed into her personal space. "The last time, I was with you. I might be kind of rusty." He watched her with hooded eyes.

"I can give you a refresher course." Elizabeth licked her lips.

The action caused him to focus on her mouth.

Henry blinked to force him to get out one last coherent thought. "If this is about trying to make me feel better—" he began.

She cut him off. "I don't want to think. Right now, all I want is you." Elizabeth grabbed his face. She kissed him hungrily.

"Which way is that shower?" Henry quipped.

They stepped into the bathroom.

Elizabeth unbuttoned her blouse. Henry's heart began to rage in his chest. He took his shirt by the hem and pulled it up over his head. He tossed it into a hamper.

He stood still studying Elizabeth's face for any sign of discomfort or fear. She answered him by taking hold of his belt and unbuckling it. They quickly finished disrobing.

Elizabeth opened the shower door and leaned in. She pulled up the shower knob. Elizabeth waited until the water warmed. She adjusted the temperature.

She reached behind her and grabbed ahold of both of Henry's hands. Elizabeth guided him in. They stopped under the stream of hot water, taking a moment to adjust to the heat. Steam enveloped them. "Your turn first," she said.

Elizabeth retrieved a body wash and squeezed some into her palm. She lathered up her hands. Starting with his neck, Elizabeth washed down his shoulders and then over to his chest. Her hands were hungry.

Henry didn't mind a bit. After she was done cleaning him, he rinsed under the spray. Their gaze stayed locked the entire time. He moved on to the places he remembered she liked to be touched. Her body arched to his feather-like fingers. She shivered as his fingers trailed down her abs.

"Turn around," Henry requested. He got more soap and then began to massage Elizabeth's neck. She moaned. Elizabeth gathered her wet hair and moved it to her front so he had better access. Slowly he massaged down her back. She closed her eyes. Having his hands on her like this again felt like magic, and Elizabeth wanted to savor every second.

Henry pulled her back to him under the stream of water. He kissed the soft skin of her shoulder. She turned around to face him.

Elizabeth hooked her arms around his neck. Henry backed her up against the wall. He lifted her up. Elizabeth wrapped her legs around his waist.

RESTORATION

The lovebirds skipped getting dressed and climbed in under the covers of the bed. The satin of the sheets stuck to their slightly damp skin. He cupped the back of her neck and drew her into his embrace. They shared several lazy kisses between smiles and laughter.

"Are you're OK?" Henry caressed her shoulders and upper arms.

"You can see I am more than OK." She glowed. "Don't worry."

"With everything you've been through—" he began.

Elizabeth pressed her pointer finger to his lips. "Believe me there is no comparison. I trust you."

"And I love you, Elizabeth," Henry crooned.

"Me too. I also love the way you always use my whole name." Elizabeth sighed contently while tracing lazy hearts into his bare chest.

"You deserve respect," he asserted. Henry joined their hands. He raised them and kissed her knuckles. Henry stared at her bare ring finger.

"Penny for your thoughts," she coaxed.

"Do you still have the ring I gave you?" he asked.

"It's safely tucked away in my jewelry box," Elizabeth answered.

His thumb stroked the base of his ring finger. "They took mine when they put me in Wonder Ridge."

"I've got something to show you." She pushed away the covers.

Henry pulled her closer. "Don't go."

"I'll be right back." She gave him a small peck as she slipped out of his hands. Elizabeth went to her dresser and opened her jewelry box. She retrieved a ring box from inside. "Here we go," Elizabeth said as she slipped back under the comforter and sheet.

"This your ring?" Henry asked.

She settled into the bed. "Open it and find out."

He snapped the lid open to find two rings in it. "His and hers." Henry smiled against the crown of her head. The circle of oval sapphires he had bought Elizabeth was there and behind it stuck his: a simple silver band.

"I found it on the floor of your studio," Elizabeth revealed. "As if they'd dropped it there to make me think you'd left."

He kissed her once again. "Shall we?"

Elizabeth nodded. She held out her hand as Henry took her ring from the box. He slid it over her knuckles. Elizabeth returned his ring to its rightful place on his ring finger.

"I wish these could be real," Henry sighed.

"They'll have to do for now." Elizabeth cuddled into him.

"Do you think we'd be getting back together after all of this if it weren't for Richard?" Henry stroked her hair.

"No," she stated. Sadness tinged her voice. He waited for her to continue. "I wouldn't be here without Richard," Elizabeth clarified.

Henry cuddled closer to her. "I guess this is fate then, huh?"

"Definitely."

She noticed the clock and frowned. "Time to get dressed." He nuzzled her nose before sitting up. Henry swung his legs over the edge of the bed. He stood and went over to the dresser for his clothes. After pulling on some boxers, Henry fished out some jeans and slid them on.

Elizabeth slipped on a white silk robe that hung on a nearby bedpost.

Little knuckles knocked on the door. "Mama?" Richard called through the barrier.

"Coming, angel." Elizabeth stood, tightening the tie of her robe. She unlocked the door and opened it.

"Hey." Elizabeth ruffled her son's hair. Richard giggled. He came inside while she waved to Jessica.

"Hey, little prince," Henry greeted sheepishly. He came over and sat on the bed.

Richard plopped down into Henry's lap. Elizabeth joined them.

"How's your face?" she inquired.

"Better," Richard said. He was getting used to the pain.

"I'm sorry if I scared you earlier, little prince," Henry said. "I saw Arthur hit you, and it made me mad at *him*. I don't want anyone to hurt you or your mom. It's not right."

"I s'ould've before I went back for Lucy." Richard hung his head.

"It was not your fault." Henry gently guided Richard's face up to his. "You are a good boy, Richard. It wasn't right that I shoved him either, but I will try to do better," Henry promised.

"You stopped Daddy," Richard's eyes shone. The word stung Henry, but he didn't let it show in his face.

"Are we cool?" Henry inquired. Richard nodded.

Henry handed Richard over to Elizabeth. She set her son in her lap. The weight transfer didn't hit her as hard as it should have. Richard felt too light for her liking. Henry's eyes locked with hers, communicating the same worry without words.

Henry got up and went back to the dresser. "I was thinking about painting some." He opened the drawer that held his painting clothes.

Elizabeth's face brightened. "Excellent." She shamelessly ogled him.

"You and Ricky want to come with?" Henry asked before pulling a paint-spattered black T-shirt over his head.

"You can go ahead and get started; I might get him a snack first," Elizabeth responded.

"Snack?" Richard placed a hand over his stomach.

"Aren't you hungry, angel?" Elizabeth inquired.

"No, Mama." Richard shook his head.

"You should eat something," she coaxed. "Maybe just some yogurt, OK?"

"I guess," Richard said.

"See you in a few." Henry craned in and kissed her soundly. Elizabeth lifted her hand and caressed his jaw before he broke the kiss.

He winked at her and then left the room. Elizabeth smiled after him. Maybe this was the breakthrough he needed.

Henry dragged his feet all the way to the door of the pool house. He closed his eyes as he reached for the doorknob. Henry inhaled and turned the knob.

Henry closed the sketch pad and moved it to the bottom shelf. He figured he'd been pushing too hard to follow an image. This time he was just going to have to wing it. Henry retrieved his palette and mixing knives. He chose two paints from their case with his eyes closed. He squeezed some of each out.

Henry launched the paintbrush like a missile across the room. He ripped the canvas off the easel. Henry slammed it into the concrete floor. Still heaving, he kicked it. The canvas sailed across the floor and under the rack of his paintings before crashing into the wall. It cluttered to the ground. The sound of its fall reverberated like thunder.

Henry surveyed the damage as tears welled in his eyes. The world began to spin around him. Henry dropped to his knees. He grabbed his hair; his arms covering his face. Henry bowed into himself, falling to the floor. His whole body ached. Every muscle racked with sobs. Henry began to rock himself.

Elizabeth threw herself over Henry. She tried to hold him still but to no avail.

A small voice broke the silence. "Ri?"

Henry sniffled as he looked up at his son. He instantly froze. Henry's heart pounded in his chest. How was he going to explain this to his son?

"You OK?" Richard asked.

The calm reaction eased Henry's nerves. "Yeah," he answered. "I ..." What could he say?

"Can I give Ri 'is present?" Richard inquired.

Elizabeth nodded her approval.

The boy scurried off to find the said gift.

Henry looked at Elizabeth questioningly. "He got it while we were shopping with Mom," she explained.

Richard settled down in front of Henry. He handed over a silver train case.

Henry looked over the case appreciatively. He found the

decorative metal plate was engraved with *HPA* in a flowing lettering. "My initials." Henry traced the letters with his fingers.

"Aren't you going to open it?" Elizabeth nudged.

Richard watched him eagerly. Henry snapped open the latches. He pulled the top apart, each bringing two shelves with them.

Inside the case was a brand-new set of paintbrushes. He ran his fingertips over the bristles. They were soft against his skin. Henry wouldn't have to break these in. It balanced well in his hand. They were high-quality brushes.

"Thank you, Ricky." He wrapped an arm around his son and pulled him in close.

"Mommy said t'ese worked for your paint," Richard replied.

Henry cleared his throat. "They are wonderful." He kissed the crown of his son's head.

"I picked t'em out," Richard reported. His chest puffed out. Henry licked his lips as they curled up into an uncontrollable smile. Pride radiated from his boy.

"He insisted on using some of his own money from his last modeling job," Elizabeth informed him.

Henry wiped the moisture off of his face with his sleeves. "We need to get off of this concrete," he said with a wet laugh. Henry stood and helped Elizabeth up.

"We can help you straighten everything," Elizabeth offered.

"You don't have to." Henry bent down and picked up the easel. He spread the legs to keep it upright. Henry looked back to his family.

Elizabeth and Richard stood right beside the portrait of

RESTORATION

Grace. Henry had to catch his breath. He straightened while inspiration hit him like a ton of bricks. For the first time in years, Henry knew exactly what he needed to paint.

Chapter Fourteen

Elizabeth woke to see Henry gazing down between them at Richard. His face soft, his eyes adored his son.

"Now this room comes with a view," she cooed.

"Hey," Henry breathed. As fast as his head went up to look at her it angled back down to Richard.

"Someone is up early," Elizabeth teased.

Henry grinned. "Today is a big day."

"I almost hate to wake him," she sighed.

Surrounded in the calm of the resort hotel room, sleep had come easily.

Henry and Elizabeth exchanged bliss-filled looks over their sleeping child's head. His eyes fluttered open slowly.

"Happy birthday, angel," Elizabeth cooed.

"Happy birthday, little prince," Henry echoed.

A wide smile spread across Richard's face. "Is it really my birthday?"

"Sure is," Henry affirmed.

"Let's go get ready. We're going to have breakfast and then on to Disneyland!" Elizabeth cheered. She got up and got their clothes out of the suitcase and then ran Richard into the bathroom.

Henry took up his clothes and got dressed in the room. There came a knock at the door. Henry answered the door and let Duncan in just as Elizabeth and Richard came out of the bathroom.

"How was your night?" Duncan inquired.

"Excellent," Elizabeth replied.

"Ricky slept great," Henry noted.

"Thanks for letting us have the night here," Elizabeth added.

"Nonsense. He deserves a full day at Disneyland," Duncan beamed.

They went down the hallway to the elevator and then made their way to the restaurant downstairs.

"What time are the reservations?" Duncan inquired.

"Eight," Henry replied.

Duncan found a guidebook to the amusement park on a display table. He picked it up and unfolded it.

"Where's my hug?"

Duncan froze. The familiar feminine voice iced the blood in his veins. He spun around slowly to see his ex-wife embracing their grandson. "How is the birthday boy today?" she inquired.

"I'm good." Richard smiled.

Elizabeth turned to Duncan with a stern glare. "Don't ruin Richard's birthday," she warned. "He loves his grandmother and wants her here."

Henry stepped forward. "Hello, Victoria." He kissed both of her cheeks.

"Suck up," Duncan muttered under his breath.

Elizabeth embraced her mother. "I'm so glad you could make it, Mom."

"I hitched a ride," Victoria quipped.

Oliver waved as he approached with Miranda, Orlando, and Ophelia.

"Uncle Ollie! Orlando! Fia!" Richard tore off toward them. He hugged Oliver first. Then Orlando and Ophelia. He held on to Ophelia as he waved to Miranda.

"How old are you today?" Oliver inquired.

Richard held up one hand showing all of his fingers. "I'm five!"

"How does it feel to be five?" Miranda inquired.

"Good!" he replied.

"Who do you think will show up?" Oliver asked the children.

"I mentioned P-e-t-e-r P-a-n, so I hope he makes an appearance," Elizabeth said.

"I'm sure he'll be thrilled with any character that shows up," Henry replied.

———

The first stop, once inside Disneyland, was the Main Street barber shop. The boys would get trims before the kids got dressed up. Miranda hovered behind Ophelia as she was getting a wig put on. Richard climbed up into the chair beside the one Orlando was getting in. Their fathers stood shoulder to shoulder behind them. The barber raised it with a push of his foot.

"How do you want your hair?" the barber inquired.

Richard pointed over to Henry. Henry pointed to himself in disbelief.

"You want it like his?" the barber asked.

Richard nodded. Elizabeth nodded her approval to the barber as well.

"OK, bud, we can do that."

Oliver grinned and nudged Henry's arm.

"How is Stephan anyway?" Duncan inquired.

Elizabeth's back stiffened.

Victoria refrained from rolling her eyes at his petty display. "*Steven* is great," she said, emphasizing her fiancé's correct name. "The FBI keeps him busy. He got called out on assignment today."

"Hope it's nothing too dangerous," Elizabeth interjected, letting both her parents know she could hear them.

"Where is Cleo?" Victoria looked around. "I thought she'd be here."

"She's comforting her sister. She's had a rough go of it lately." Duncan pressed his lips together in a forced smile.

"That's too bad," Victoria replied before returning her attention to the birthday boy.

The barber showed Richard his haircut in the mirror. "What do you think?" he inquired.

Richard looked from Henry to the mirror. "Great!"

The barber brushed off his neck. He let down the chair and Richard hopped off. Elizabeth held her breath as she looked between her father and Henry. With Richard and Henry having the same haircut and matching outfits, the resemblance was unmistakable.

"Are you ready for your new outfits?" the cast member asked enthusiastically.

"Yeah!" the kids agreed in unison.

"All right, we've got a place for you to change right in the back," she directed.

"Can Ri take me?" Richard asked.

"Sure, angel," Elizabeth agreed. "We'll wait out here."

Henry, Oliver, and Miranda disappeared with the kids into the back. Elizabeth used the time to retrieve a blue ribbon from her purse. Elizabeth tied the ribbon into a bow in her hair. She smoothed down her powder-blue baby doll dress. "Think Richard will notice?"

"I think he'll get the reference," Victoria replied.

The guys came back with the boys as Miranda returned with Ophelia.

"I look like Peter Pan!" Richard giggled as he spun around. He stopped cold in front of his mother. Richard looked Elizabeth over. "Are you Wendy, Mama?" he asked. Elizabeth nodded brightly. "Wow!" Richard beamed, taking her by the hand.

"And who are you?" Oliver asked his daughter.

"I'm a pirate!" Ophelia laughed.

Miranda shook her head. "I tried to get her in the Tinkerbell costume."

"I wanna be a pirate!" Ophelia replied.

"That's my girl," Oliver chuckled.

Miranda gave him the side eye before playfully nudging him with her elbow. Oliver kissed her check. "She has all the princess dresses at home and uses them frequently," he reminded her. Oliver took the hat from Miranda's hands and placed it on Ophelia's head.

"Now who's ready to go check out some rides?" Duncan rubbed his hands together.

RESTORATION

Oliver picked up his glass as he let out a laugh. Elizabeth laid her head on Henry's shoulder and contently watched the kids eat. A cast member dressed as Peter Pan walked in and approached their table. Richard's jaw dropped to the floor.

"Peter?" Richard gasped.

Henry took up the camera from around his neck. He snapped off the moment as the actor playing Peter approached Richard.

"My friend Tink told me someone at this table is having a birthday today." The cast member smiled.

"Me." Richard raised his hand.

"And what's your name?" Peter asked.

"I'm Richard."

"How about a picture?" Henry requested.

Peter nodded. Richard got down from his chair. He knelt on one knee and wrapped an arm around Richard's shoulder. The boy couldn't help grinning. His heart just about leaped out of his chest. Henry craned down for the proper angle and took multiple pictures.

"Now everybody." Peter motioned with both of his hands for the other kids.

Ophelia and Orlando gathered around. Henry snapped off several more shots.

Just then, servers brought out the dessert. The kids were quickly ushered back to their seats. The cast member joined them in singing "Happy Birthday" to Richard.

"Make a wish," Peter directed.

Richard sucked in all the air his little lungs could hold. He blew out the candles with one breath. Everyone clapped. The cake was sliced and divvied out.

"Have a magical evening!" The cast member waved as he exited.

Richard waved back until he couldn't see him. He stared in awe at his cake; marveling at the toppers. "The first piece is for the birthday boy," Duncan insisted.

Elizabeth set the plate in front of Richard. He took up his fork and took a bite. "Mmmm."

"Is it good?" Henry asked.

"Yummy chocolate," Richard bubbled.

After the party, they returned to their hotel room. The staff had already set up Richard's pile of gifts on a coffee table in the sitting area. Beyond the gift bags and beautifully wrapped boxes sat a medium-sized fabric-covered object.

"What is that?" Victoria whispered pointing to something cloth-covered in the back.

"Something Henry painted for Richard," Elizabeth whispered.

Victoria grinned. "A new painting?"

"Henry hasn't even let me see it yet." Elizabeth smiled in return. "He worked nonstop on it for two days."

Richard picked up the first brightly colored box. He ripped open the paper to lift open the lid. Inside Richard found the Dodger's cap Henry had bought him. Richard traded his Peter Pan hat for the cap.

The mitt was hidden under the hat. Richard picked it up.

"It's like yours, but smaller," he marveled.

"Slip it on," Henry urged.

Richard complied. He found the leather a bit stiff, but he got it open. "You'll need to work it a bit," Henry encouraged. "You can use it when we play catch."

"I bet Henry hasn't told you yet, but we played on the same baseball team," Oliver offered.

"Really?" Richard tilted his head.

"Did he tell you he was the star pitcher on our team?" Oliver nudged his friend.

"No," Richard replied.

"He had a killer arm, this one," Oliver reported.

"So does Ricky," Henry praised. Richard beamed and puffed out his chest.

"You gonna grow up to be a pitcher?" Oliver asked.

"Maybe," Richard shrugged.

"I always wondered why you didn't go the professional route with that," Oliver questioned his friend.

"While I love the game, I was in it for my full ride to SoCal," Henry said.

Richard set the glove aside but kept the cap. He had more presents to open.

The next few gifts were from Elizabeth and then Duncan. Richard yanked up on the ribbon handles of a gift bag and brought it out front.

He pointed to the tag on it. Elizabeth read it for him. "This is from Nonna."

Richard tossed aside the tissue paper and pulled out Peter Pan and Wendy plush dolls.

"T'ank you, Nonna." Richard squeezed his new toys.

"Now Lucy has a few friends." Victoria smiled.

Richard picked up a small garment box next. His parents had skipped the tape while wrapping so the lid came off easily. He folded the paper to each side to find the Dodgers' jersey. "Wow," Richard exclaimed. He slid it on over his new costume.

"It's just your size," Elizabeth said approvingly.

"Looks like you're all set for this one," Oliver said. He picked up a thin, rectangular box and handed it to Richard. Richard lifted the lid. Two tickets. He couldn't read the printed information. On the end of it, he saw a clue as to what they were.

"Dodgers' logo," Richard mused.

"They're tickets for their next home game," Oliver explained. "We thought you might enjoy seeing a game in person."

Richard looked up at Duncan with big blue eyes. "Can I, Granddad?" The boy batted his lashes.

Duncan glanced over to Oliver. Oliver winked at the older man. Duncan had to give it to the actor. Oliver played things on the sly.

"We'll make sure you can," Duncan answered.

"T'ank you, Uncle Ollie," Richard said.

"OK, last one." Henry motioned to the cloth-covered canvas.

"T'at's for me?" Richard questioned.

"It sure is." Henry nodded.

Richard raised the covering cloth and tossed it to the side. The blue and green gradient background and other coloring aspects were similar to Henry's painting of Grace, but it was Elizabeth's portrait. Richard let out a squeal.

"Mama, look! Ri painted you!"

Richard reached up toward Henry. Henry lifted his son into a hug. "T'ank you! T'ank you, Ri!" Richard threw his arms around Henry's neck.

"You're very welcome, buddy." Henry smiled.

"I love it!" Richard said. Henry kissed Richard's temple and set him back on his feet.

"Look, Granddad! It's Mama!" Richard clapped.

"It certainly is," Duncan replied.

Fireworks came and went. Oliver and his family said their goodnights and left. Richard yawned.

"It is way past your bedtime," Elizabeth noted.

"Goodnight, Granddad."

"Rest well, I have more presents for you at home tomorrow," Duncan promised.

Richard hugged Victoria. "Good night, Nonna."

"Goodnight, birthday boy." She kissed his forehead. "I hope you had a great day."

"I did. T'ank you for coming," Richard replied.

Victoria took his face in her hands and nuzzled his nose.

The former couple was left alone on the balcony. They shifted where they sat, looking anywhere but at each other.

Duncan licked his lips and cleared his throat. "This was a good day."

"Richard and Elizabeth enjoyed themselves," Victoria agreed. "You probably had something to do with Peter Pan showing up."

"Maybe I made a phone call or two." He pursed his lips.

"Thank you for that," she said.

"Arthur would have loved to come," Duncan remarked.

"At least he had the decency to give Richard a stress-free birthday," Victoria acknowledged.

"Things could have gotten tense with Henry here too," Duncan admitted.

"After everything you and Arthur put him through can you blame him?" she scoffed.

"Even Elizabeth has a part in this," he asserted.

"She married the wrong man. I did that once." Victoria straightened her shoulders.

Duncan took a large swallow of his drink, trying not to feel the sting of her words.

"At least I did it out of love instead of fear," she added.

"What is that supposed to mean?" he leaned back in his chair. "I don't do riddles; they are a tedious waste of time."

"I know how you forced Lizzie to marry Arthur," she leveled.

Duncan locked eyes with his ex-wife. "That's harsh."

"That's exactly what you did," Victoria returned.

"I gave Lizzie a push in the right direction," he deflected.

"So that's what you call this?" she reached into her purse and produced a Polaroid. He held up his hand. Victoria set it in her lap for the time being. "Elizabeth received it not two days before she married Arthur."

"Why are we getting into this now?" Duncan swirled the liquid in his glass.

She locked eyes with him. "Because I also know you have them back at the mansion."

"Vicki," he crooned.

"Stop," she directed. "You do not get to call me that

anymore."

"Is that Steve's nickname for you?" Duncan huffed.

"I feel the same way about that name as Steven does about being called *Steve*." Victoria rolled her eyes.

"You didn't complain about the name when we were married," Duncan replied.

"You are trying to get us off subject," she said.

"Which is?" He raised an eyebrow.

"I'm concerned about Liz and Richard's wellbeing." Victoria leaned forward and rested on her elbows.

"Everything is fine," Duncan asserted.

"Arthur is still living there, isn't he?" She narrowed her hazel eyes at him. Duncan pushed out his bottom lip and raised his shoulders. "I'll take that as a yes," Victoria said.

"So what?" Duncan frowned.

"Need I remind you we almost lost Richard only six months ago." She cocked her head.

"I was there," he grumbled.

"I can't believe you are tolerating anyone harming our grandson," Victoria inhaled. She could still hear her daughter's anguished screams from six months before.

"It was a one-time incident. It will not happen again," Duncan assured her.

"As much sway as you hold over Arthur, you can't promise he won't hurt them," Victoria asserted. "Has Arthur hurt either of them since they've been back? Don't try to sell me any bull. I will get a straight answer from Elizabeth." Victoria cocked her head.

Duncan downplayed it. "A little discipline got out of hand with Richard. But as you can see he's fine."

"'Discipline.'" She used air quotes as she repeated the

word.

"Don't be so dramatic." He waved her concern off.

"It's pretty clear he can't control himself, and you are forcing our grandson to be around him?" Victoria questioned incredulously.

"Elizabeth is doing a fine job of keeping them apart all on her own." Duncan frowned.

"I'd be doing the same damn thing if I were her," Victoria retorted.

"You would have kept Lizzie away from me?" he questioned.

"It's not the same thing. You were never violent with us." Victoria licked her lips. She nodded her head sheepishly. "I have to admit despite our rocky times I'd describe you as affectionate," Victoria added.

"Things weren't all bad, were they?" Duncan tipped his head.

"Even when you took Liz from me I never doubted you loved her," she continued.

Duncan's brow furrowed. "You do now?"

"It's not what I think you should worry about," Victoria answered. "Your misguided attempts to corral Liz into your version of a perfect life could destroy your relationship with her."

"I'm misguided?" Duncan threw his head back.

"It's not a healthy situation for anyone," she argued.

"Lizzie requires a firmer hand than you," he countered.

"What about Richard? He's just a boy," Victoria questioned.

"Who needs his father," Duncan asserted.

She mentally counted to ten. Victoria had serious doubts

concerning Arthur's claims in that arena. Her suspicions were all but confirmed seeing Henry interact with Richard. "Not one that terrorizes him. Do you think if something happens to Richard that Liz will up and have another kid?" she scoffed. "We both know it's not always that easy."

He shrugged. "Lizzie made her choice."

"She didn't choose you or Arthur: Liz chose to save Henry," Victoria asserted.

"What did Henry need saving from?" Duncan scoffed.

"You." She shoved the Polaroid into Duncan's face. He yanked it from her hand to hold it out of sight. Duncan didn't need to see it to know what the image showed: Henry forced to his stomach, tied up, and gagged. Someone out of range of the camera held a gun to his head.

Duncan frowned. "Where did you get this?"

"I took it to keep Liz from obsessing over it." Victoria raised her head.

He scrunched up his face. "She told you?"

"She came to her mother, completely freaked out," she clarified.

"Don't expect me to apologize for trying to guide my daughter," he snapped.

"Paying someone to do this to Henry is a pretty clear threat on his life," Victoria argued.

"They cut him loose." Duncan rubbed an eyebrow.

Her lip curled back. "Like that makes it all OK?"

"He's still around." He finished his drink.

Victoria nodded her head. "Henry's taken a ton of crap from you to be with Liz."

"Have you joined the Henry fan club now?" Duncan huffed.

"I don't have to, our daughter adores him," Victoria said.

"That shouldn't be the only requirement—" he began.

She cut him off. "I'll never understand what you see in Arthur or why you want Liz with him."

"How is it so hard to see I am trying to give her some stability?" he insisted.

"There's no stability with him." Victoria placed a hand on his shoulder. Duncan tensed at her touch. "If you love them you'll set them free," she insisted.

"To be with a painter who can't possibly take care of them?" His upper lip curled.

"Why are you so threatened by Henry?" Victoria questioned.

Duncan laughed.

"You're only laughing because it's true," she charged. Victoria stood without another word and went inside.

He stared off into the night sky mulling over Victoria's accusations. She didn't know the half of it.

Chapter Fifteen

Henry opened the refrigerator door. He selected a beer. Twisting around, he gave it to Oliver.

"Why do I feel like my mom is going to walk in and bust us?" Oliver quipped.

"We better get out of here before the cook shows up to start dinner." Henry grabbed one for himself. He closed the door and they headed out to the living room.

"So are we going to talk about these dreams you mentioned?" Oliver asked.

Henry chuckled and scratched one of his eyebrows. "Yeah …"

"Hey, it's just us guys here. You can unload on me," Oliver encouraged.

"Be careful what you ask for," Henry replied.

"It's hard to scare me," Oliver reassured.

"I'm the violent one in them. In the last one, I took a baseball bat to Arthur." Henry shook his head.

Oliver frowned. It wasn't like his friend to wish harm on another person even under the most justifiable circumstances.

"I know I sound—"

Oliver cut him off. "Angry. Does that about sum it up?"

"Putting a pounding on the punching bag can do wonders." Oliver smiled.

The back door opened. Elizabeth ushered Richard inside.

"There you two are." Oliver smiled.

"Hi, Uncle Ollie." Richard waved.

Elizabeth crossed to the couch. She leaned over and gave Henry a kiss.

"I see someone is wearing his jersey." Oliver smirked.

"He's going to live in it if we let him." Elizabeth mussed Richard's hair.

They hear a phone ring. A few moments later, Felix appeared. "Your agent is on the phone," Felix informed Elizabeth.

"I'll take it upstairs," she said. Felix nodded and left. "Are you gonna come with me, angel?" Elizabeth offered.

"You can stay with us guys if you want," Henry offered.

Elizabeth picked up the phone on her nightstand. "What's shaking, Drew?" She smiled at the framed picture of her guys that sat beside the phone.

"I got off the phone with Filmores," Drew answered.

"And?" Elizabeth questioned.

"They appreciate you wearing their dress to Spring Fire's opening."

She chuckled. "I figured I'd make the best of the situation."

"They want you to shoot a commercial," Drew added.

"That might be doable. You know my schedule," Elizabeth

agreed.

"I'll set it up." The agent nodded his head. "Tristian also called."

"About the swimsuit shoot?" Elizabeth deduced.

"How did you know? Did he talk to you about it already?" Drew replied.

"I'd love to go, but I don't think I'll be able to take my son," Elizabeth declined. As if on cue, Richard bounded into the room and picked up his Peter Pan plush.

She heard footsteps on the stairs.

"It's OK. I've got him, Henry," she called.

Elizabeth frowned when the steps kept coming. She turned around to lock her door. Arthur was already inside the room. Her stomach fell.

"Turn right around," Elizabeth pointed out into the hall.

"We need to talk," Arthur said.

"I'm busy, Arthur." Elizabeth pointed to the phone in her hand.

"Is everything OK?" Drew questioned.

"Sorry, Drew, what was that?"

"Tell your agent you have to go," Arthur insisted.

He reached down and hit the phone plunger. Arthur kept himself between her and the door.

"Say your piece and get out." Elizabeth crossed her arms over her chest.

"We need to revisit the discussion of us having a kid," he insisted.

She laughed. "No."

"Things have changed. You have Henry back." Arthur put his hands on his hips.

"I won't repeat myself on this subject." She threw her

hands up.

"Don't be so childish," he entreated.

"Says the man who gets jealous of a five-year-old!" Elizabeth retorted.

"I am not jealous," Arthur denied.

"Oliver," Duncan chirped.

The men sitting on the couch angled to see the source of the noise. Duncan came further into the room. "Neither of your kids came with you?"

"This isn't such a good place for kids," Oliver replied. "Richard is more than welcome over to my house anytime."

"Did you figure out where to hang the portrait?" Duncan asked.

"He wanted it with my mom's out in the pool house," Henry answered.

"Really? I would have sworn he'd want it in his room." Duncan slipped off his suit jacket.

"He doesn't really spend any time in there." Henry frowned.

"You could use it as an incentive for him to grow up a little," Duncan advised. "Or do you want him sleeping in his mother's bed?"

"It's probably the safest place for him at night," Oliver interjected.

Duncan scrunched up his face. He tilted his head back as if in challenge. "You don't live here."

"I've heard and seen plenty." Oliver kept up the eye

contact.

"History doesn't have to repeat itself," Duncan replied.

"If someone treated my daughter, just once, the way you allow Arthur to treat yours, my foot would be so far up his ass it would have to be surgically removed," Oliver asserted.

"Dad used to shower you with attention and praise before Richard was born," Elizabeth pressed.

Arthur nodded. "He did."

"And now he's turned aloof? Even downright mean sometimes?" she needled.

He pressed his lips together.

"Welcome to my world! The same exact thing happened to me when you showed up," Elizabeth sneered.

"Things would be different if we actually gave him what he really wants," Arthur asserted.

"We can't give him a son," she retorted.

Arthur set his shoulders. "You know what I mean."

"He has a grandson," Elizabeth countered.

Arthur's gray eyes shot daggers in Richard's direction. Elizabeth stepped between them. "Hey, leave him alone." She snapped her fingers to break Arthur's focus.

"He's the reason you keep saying no," he rejoined.

"It's more about me than him," Elizabeth admitted.

"Go ahead and blow your smoke, old man. It doesn't mean I'll be listening." Oliver took a swig of his beer.

"While I admire your loyalty, your taste in friends leaves something to be desired." Duncan's lips curled back.

"Were you the one that carried me out to help when I broke my leg during our sophomore field trip?" Oliver raised an eyebrow in challenge. "Or did you risk incurring Miranda's wrath by offering to drive the getaway car when I got cold feet right before my wedding?" He waited for a response but none came. "No? I didn't think so."

"You young ones have to learn the hard way, don't you?" Duncan scoffed.

"What is your deal tonight?" Henry frowned.

"I'm just stating the obvious," Duncan replied.

"You may hate me, and that's fine, but it's not cool to try and bully my friends," the younger man stood.

"I never said I hated you," Duncan countered.

"You don't have to. Funny thing is, I don't think we really had a problem until I asked Elizabeth to marry me," Henry said.

Duncan's eyes flicked down to Henry's left hand.

"You think that ring makes you special," Duncan scoffed. "It means nothing to everyone else."

"Lucky 'everyone else' isn't important," Henry replied.

"Just Lizzie and Ricky matter, right? Nice little niche you found for yourself. Richard sees you as his protector," Duncan snorted.

"Someone has to protect him," Oliver chimed in.

"You're his hero now." Duncan didn't divert his attention from Henry.

"You'd be too if you stepped in," Henry rejoined.

RESTORATION

———

Richard covered his ears as the two grownups' voices got louder.

"Please, you're just as self-absorbed as he is!" Elizabeth retorted.

Arthur grabbed her arm. He got in her face. "Have some respect!" Arthur growled.

Frightened, Richard ran out of the room.

"How about the two of you earn some?" She yanked her arm free.

"We made a deal," Arthur argued.

"You have broken every part of the deal," Elizabeth charged. "We owe you nothing!"

"You wouldn't even consider adding to the agreement," Arthur countered.

"I can't do what you are asking. I will not, cannot do that to Henry," she declared.

"If he is in love with you as deeply as you think it won't matter to him," Arthur asserted.

"Henry has asked for another kid," Elizabeth embellished.

"And what did you tell him?" Arthur demanded.

"Let me put this in terms you can understand: I am only having Henry's kids," she asserted. They stood there in silent stalemate for more than a minute. Elizabeth straightened her shoulders. "Now I am going to go find my son. Do not be here when we get back," she instructed.

He stretched his arms across the doorframe, blocking her exit.

"Let me out," she demanded. She had seen that rage in his

eyes before.

Elizabeth attempted to duck under his arm. He caught her by the neck. Arthur lifted her off of her feet. They traveled up over the bed. He slammed her between the bedposts into the wall. The impact knocked the air out of her. Elizabeth's eyes darted around the room. She clawed at his hands. Her nails scraped deep into his skin, but it didn't faze him. Elizabeth kicked at him with all her strength, but it was like fighting a brick wall.

"Arthur has his flaws," Duncan acknowledged.

"He's an abusive wipe and you know it," Henry sneered.

"How you do think he feels seeing you with his family?" Duncan snarled.

"Arthur doesn't love them and sure as hell doesn't want them!" Henry thundered.

"And you? You love them, you want them," Duncan challenged.

"Yes!" Henry yelled. He wanted no mistake about that.

"Even though he's Arthur's son?" Duncan threw back.

It took all Henry had inside him not to yell out the truth. "Richard is a part of Elizabeth! And I love all of Elizabeth," Henry proclaimed.

Richard came into the room screaming at the top of his lungs, "Ri!"

"What's wrong, little prince?" Henry asked.

"Daddy's going to 'urt Mama!" Richard tugged at Henry's hand.

"Where is your mom?" Henry inquired.

"Our room!"

"Stay with Uncle Ollie," Henry directed. He took off like a rocket, flying up through the house and up the stairs. "Elizabeth!" Henry yelled as his feet reached the landing.

He came into the room just in time to see Elizabeth go limp.

Henry rammed into Arthur, causing the other man to lose his grip and knocking him to the floor. Without Arthur holding her upright, Elizabeth slumped over. Ignoring Arthur, Henry went to check on her. "Elizabeth," he stroked her face. "Elizabeth!" Henry cried. He kissed both of her cheeks.

Henry laid his head on her chest. He held his breath and listened for any noise. His heart dropped. No heartbeat, nothing, not a sound.

Duncan entered the doorway. He was so shocked at the sight of Elizabeth lying lifeless on the floor that he didn't see Arthur run out of the room. Richard wasn't too far behind his granddad. He had moved too fast for Oliver to stop him.

"Call 911," Henry ordered.

Oliver reached the phone and dialed before Duncan did.

"911, what is your emergency?"

"Please, send the police and an ambulance out to 555 Sanders Drive," Oliver said. "My friend was just attacked by her estranged husband. He's choked her."

"Is she breathing?" the operator asked.

"No," Henry continued with the chest compressions.

"She's not breathing," Oliver relayed. "One of my other friends is doing CPR."

"Get up, Mama," Richard pleaded.

"Oliver, get Richard out of here!" Henry ordered. He

continued alternating giving Elizabeth breaths and doing chest compressions while praying silently. *Please, give her back. Don't let her die in front of Richard.*

Elizabeth's eyes popped open. She gasped violently for air.

"Elizabeth?" Henry crooned.

She lifted her hand and touched his cheek. "Thank God." He angled his face to kiss her palm. Elizabeth opened her mouth. She tried to form words, but only garbled, nearly inaudible sounds came out. Elizabeth frowned. "Hey, hey, hey, take it easy, babe," Henry cooed.

The EMTs rushed in. Henry helped her sit up. The responders checked her vital signs.

"Are you in any pain?" one of the EMTs asked.

Elizabeth patted her neck.

"You can't talk?" the EMT deduced. "OK, can you show me where you are in pain?" he inquired.

Elizabeth flattened her hand and made a circle going down from her neck into the top her ribs.

"Why can't she speak?" Duncan asked.

"The doctors will be able to tell you more when they find out the extent of the trauma." The EMT turned his attention back to Elizabeth. "We're going to load you in and transport you to a hospital for some scans, OK?"

"Of course," Henry answered for her. He turned determined eyes to Duncan. "She's going to the hospital," Henry insisted.

Elizabeth squeezed his arm.

"We'll see what we can do about your neck."

Richard peeked his head into the room. Elizabeth held out her arms toward her son. Richard understood immediately and ran into his mother's embrace. After the reassurance, Richard was transferred over to Henry's lap so the EMTs could finish looking her over.

"You did good, buddy." Henry rubbed Richard's back. He kissed the crown of Richard's head. "You did real good."

"OK, we're ready." The EMT put his penlight back in his pocket.

"Can he ride with her?" Henry requested.

The EMT looked between the mother and child. "He'll be in my lap the entire time," Henry promised.

"I don't see the harm," the EMT replied.

"We'll follow in my car," Oliver said.

"I wanna stay with Mama," Richard whimpered. He stared off in the direction his mother had been wheeled.

"We'll get back to see her soon," Henry soothed him. He knelt down in front of his son.

"Now!"

"Soon. The special machines need time to see inside Mama's neck to see if anything inside is hurt," Henry explained.

"Is she *ouwed* on the inside?" Richard questioned.

"I don't know, but if she is, the doctors can fix it," Henry encouraged. Richard's sniffles gave way to sobs. Henry picked him up and began to rock him.

Oliver and Duncan joined them in the waiting area.

"Where is she?" Duncan demanded.

"They took her to imaging," Henry answered. He angled

his head to kiss Richard's forehead.

"Is she OK?" Oliver asked.

"So far so good," Henry said.

"You're not thinking of running, are you?" Duncan challenged.

Henry raised an eyebrow. "Elizabeth and Richard are my number-one priority."

"I invented the avoidance answer." Duncan crossed his arms over his chest.

"Can we just focus on taking care of Elizabeth?" Henry snapped.

"Did they tell you how long they expect the scans to take?" Duncan asked. "I can take Richard now." Duncan held out his hands.

"I want Ri!" Richard insisted. Duncan reached out for him. Henry turned, getting Richard out of Duncan's reach. Duncan went around to get at Richard. Richard began to kick backward at the person trying to remove him from Henry. "Ri! Ri!" Richard shouted.

"It's your granddad, Ricky," Duncan coaxed.

"Just stop." Henry tightened his grip. "He is fine where he is." He turned again.

Duncan sighed and retracted his hands. He placed them on his hips.

Henry rubbed Richard's back. "I've got you," he promised.

Henry sat down with Richard. Oliver sat beside them. Duncan chose a chair across the aisle. None of them spoke as the people milled around them. They soon became accustomed to the sounds of the hospital.

Before thirty minutes were out, a nurse approached.

"Ms. Harper is asking for her son," the nurse said.

Henry indicated the boy in his arms. "This is Richard."

"Where is Mama?" Richard asked.

The nurse craned down to look Richard in the eye. "If you'll follow me, I will take you to her room," she offered.

Henry nodded. They headed for the elevator along with Oliver. Duncan followed a step or two behind.

When they arrived at Elizabeth's room, two police officers were interviewing the patient. Elizabeth wrote her answers on a large notepad. Henry set Richard down. The five-year-old immediately climbed onto the foot of the bed. Elizabeth held out her arms. He crawled into her lap. She hugged him tight. Henry craned down and kissed her forehead. Elizabeth scooted over. He sat next to her and wrapped an arm around her shoulders.

A man in a lab coat came in. "Hello, Ms. Harper, I'm Dr. Fritz," he introduced himself. "I've gone over your scans and would like to discuss my findings with you." Though it was painful, Elizabeth nodded. "Your hyoid bone is cracked, along with a few ribs, also there is some swelling in the trachea and the surrounding tissue, impeding the vocal cords."

"Is that why she can't speak?" Henry asked.

The doctor nodded. "In a few days, the swelling should go down."

Elizabeth wrote on her pad and showed it to Dr. Fritz.

"Yeah, that's the idea," he said.

"So she's all checked out now? Can we take her home?" Duncan inquired.

The doctors saw the occupants of the bed tense. "I'd really like to keep her overnight for observation," he insisted.

Henry knew what the doctor was doing but looked

Elizabeth in the eyes. "Better safe than sorry, right?"

Elizabeth scribbled down an *OK*.

"We'll be giving you some pain medication to ease the discomfort," Dr. Fritz said. "I'll be in to check on you again."

"Thank you, Doctor." Henry shook his hand.

"Since you are stuck here for the night, can I get you anything?" Duncan offered. Elizabeth flipped over the piece of paper. Her pen flew over the new page. She turned it around for Duncan to read: *Lucy. She'll help Ricky sleep.*

"You're planning to keep Ricky here?" Duncan's brow furrowed.

Elizabeth wrote in big block letters: *MY SON IS STAYING WITH ME.*

"You don't want to spend all night in a hospital room, do you?" Duncan asked his grandson.

"I want to stay with Mama," Richard insisted.

Henry caught Oliver's eyes and then motioned with his head toward Elizabeth and Richard. Oliver nodded to acknowledge the unspoken communication. Henry took Duncan by the shoulder and stepped out of the room with him.

"Stop making this harder for them," Henry chided. "A young child seeing his mother die right in front of him? That is a moment that never leaves you." His voice was thick. "I should know."

"You were there when your mother passed?" Duncan's eyes widened.

Henry cast his eyes to the floor and nodded. "We had a few kind neighbors that made sure I was with her until the end."

"You think you know what Ricky is going through?" Duncan questioned.

"Mom's death wasn't violent, but it was terrifying in and of itself." Henry swallowed.

"I can't imagine," Duncan said.

"Richard is scared out of his mind. Separating him from Elizabeth right now would be cruel," Henry insisted.

One of the detectives who had been speaking with Elizabeth came out of the room. "Mr. Angevin? May I speak with you for a moment?"

"Certainly," Henry agreed.

The detective motioned to a set of chairs. Henry could see Elizabeth and Richard through the window.

"Can you tell me what happened?"

"I was downstairs with my friend Oliver," Henry answered.

"The man that made the second 911 call?"

Henry nodded. "Duncan came home and the three of us got talking. Richard came running to me, screaming that Arthur was hurting Elizabeth."

"Just for clarity's sake, when you say 'Arthur,' you are referring to...?"

"Arthur Corbin," Henry confirmed.

"What happened next?"

"I ran to Elizabeth's room," Henry recounted. "When I got there, Arthur had his hands around Elizabeth's neck. I knocked him off of her and he ran away. She wasn't breathing, so I performed CPR. Luckily, I was able to revive her."

"What is your relationship to Ms. Harper?" the cop asked.

Henry's eyes flicked up over the officer's shoulder where Duncan was watching him. "I'm her boyfriend," he answered.

"Thank you for your time, Mr. Angevin." The officer held out a card to Henry. "If you can think of anything else, please, give me a call."

Henry took the card and nodded.

The detective walked away. "What the hell was that, Henry?" Duncan snapped.

Henry stood. "The truth. I told you I am done with being discreet."

Duncan saw Victoria stomping toward them. He could feel the fire she was breathing from all the way down the hall. He froze. Victoria walked up to him and without a word slapped him across his face. His head went to the side and he stumbled back a good three feet before regaining his balance. Duncan placed his hand over his now burning skin. "How could you let this happen!" Victoria accused.

"I had no idea—" Duncan began.

"Where is my daughter?" she cut him off. Henry held out his hand to the door of Elizabeth's room.

"How did you ...?" Duncan questioned.

"Oliver called me. I can't count on you to even let me know my baby nearly died!" Victoria charged.

"There wasn't time," Duncan protested.

"Forget it!" She held her hand up and marched past him. Henry followed Elizabeth's mother. He continued inside while Victoria paused in the doorway. "It might be smart for you to wait out here," she directed.

Duncan watched through the window as Victoria hugged Elizabeth and Richard. She stroked her daughter's hair. Duncan took a deep breath. How was he going to fix this?

Chapter Sixteen

D uncan shuffled along the hospital hallway. He shifted the bag he carried over his shoulder. Hopefully things had cooled off overnight. Duncan knocked on the door before going in.

"Good morning, Ricky," Duncan greeted. Richard got up and gave Duncan's leg a tepid squeeze. Duncan patted Richard's back. He reached in the top of the bag. "Look who came with me." Duncan pulled out Peter Pan plush.

Richard took the toy and then slinked off to Henry. A heave of his stomach caused him to bark out a gagging cough. Henry picked him up and sat him on his lap. Richard sagged against Henry.

"Are you feeling OK?" Duncan inquired.

Henry frowned. "His stomach is torn to shreds." He laid his cheek on Richard's hair.

"I t'rew up," Richard reported, his arms wrapped around his abdomen.

"Can't the doctors give him something to settle his stomach?" Duncan asked.

"They did." Elizabeth frowned. "And then he threw that

up too." She looked over at Henry. "We might need to take him down to PEDs," Elizabeth directed. Henry nodded in agreement. Richard was acting too much like a ragdoll for his father's liking.

"Your voice came back." Duncan smiled. It was weak, but she could talk.

"I suppose it has," she replied.

"I brought some clothes for you." Duncan set the bag down on a chair. He looked around the room. Henry rubbed his eyes. With the way Richard was acting and the shadows on Elizabeth's face, Duncan wagered there hadn't been a lot of sleeping going on last night.

"Knock, knock," Oliver called. Ophelia came strolling into the room, leading Oliver in by the hand.

"Hi, Uncle Henry," Ophelia greeted.

"Hi there, Ophelia," Henry replied.

"How are you feeling?" Oliver inquired.

"I'm better," Elizabeth replied.

The young girl patted Richard's hand. Richard perked up the moment her hand touched his hand. "Fia!" Richard got down off of Henry's knee.

Ophelia gave him a huge hug. "Want to play? I brought toys." She pointed to the backpack Oliver carried on one shoulder.

"OK," Richard answered brightly.

Oliver slipped the bag down into his hand and gave it to Ophelia.

"Why don't you bring those up here?" Elizabeth offered them the end of the bed.

The two children skipped over.

Henry mouthed a thank-you to Oliver. Oliver tipped his

head.

"Sorry you hurt, Aunt Liz," the little girl said.

"Thank you, sweetheart. I'm getting better," Elizabeth replied.

"When are they releasing you?" Duncan inquired.

"Some time this morning." She rubbed her neck. It was discolored purple in two hand-shaped bruises across her windpipe. She settled back into the bed with a hiss.

"Isn't that a good thing?" he smiled.

"Where are we going to go?" Elizabeth shrugged.

"You are coming to stay with us," Oliver insisted.

She began to decline. "That's very generous of you."

"We have the rooms. The kids adore each other," Oliver cut her off.

"I'm sure Miranda would love that." Elizabeth rolled her eyes.

"She understands the situation." Oliver patted her hand. His eyes flicked to Duncan. The older man saw that he wanted to say something more.

"You're not going to let the cops find Arthur." Elizabeth snorted.

"I will deal with him," Duncan vowed.

"Like you did after he nearly killed Richard?" Henry scoffed. "How well did that work?"

Duncan scowled at Henry.

"He learned nothing. There were no consequences," Henry fumed.

"Maybe we should take a walk," Duncan suggested.

"I'm not so sure that is a good idea," Henry objected.

"A lap around the ward."

"I'll be back," Elizabeth promised.

Henry kissed her mouth boldly, not caring what Duncan thought. Henry locked eyes with her. "I love you."

"Me too," she replied. Elizabeth got up and joined her father.

Henry leveled a warning glare in Duncan's direction as the two left.

"I guess he really is your knight in shining armor now." Duncan sighed.

"Father, Henry saved my life last night," she pointed out.

"I know he did and I'm grateful." He lowered his head. "I wish it hadn't been necessary."

"Better it happened to me than Richard," Elizabeth sighed. They continued to stroll along for a minute before speaking again.

"What are you going to do about Arthur?" she asked.

"I haven't decided yet," Duncan admitted.

"Is this the part where you tell me Arthur didn't mean it, that he needs help—" Elizabeth started.

He shook his head. "I know better."

"OK, what do you want to talk about?" she queried.

"Why were the two of you fighting?" Duncan asked.

Elizabeth stopped cold. "What difference does that make?" She scowled.

"My head isn't quite wrapping around last night," he explained.

"The last thing I said to him was 'let me out'," she said. "That's all you need to know."

"I'm sorry," Duncan said.

Elizabeth inhaled sharply. "Look, I understand that Arthur is the son you've always wanted and therefore infinitely more valuable than me."

"Lizzie ..." Duncan pinched the bridge of his nose.

"Being around Arthur is not healthy for your grandson." Elizabeth shook her head.

"Arthur is his father," he protested.

"Arthur is a man who tried to kill him and then his mother," she retorted.

"You think you can just give Richard a replacement father?" Duncan frowned.

"Henry isn't some random guy," Elizabeth pushed back.

"Like that makes it any better." He slammed his hands into his pockets.

"You'll never get me, will you?" she lamented.

"Help me understand why you're holding on to Henry when you should be thinking about your child." Duncan shook his head.

"Richard is my world, and Henry is my heart," Elizabeth professed.

"You've got no room for anyone else," he returned.

"Nothing is taking their place or yours." She squeezed his arm.

"You never gave Arthur a chance," Duncan remarked.

"You're giving him enough chances for both of us. You already got him off once, what's another attempted murder charge?" she remarked.

"Watch your tone, Elizabeth Candace," Duncan commanded.

"It's you whose tone needs adjusting!" Henry growled.

They both looked over to find Henry in the doorway of Elizabeth's room. He held out his arm to help guide her back inside.

"Who the hell do you think you are?" Duncan challenged.

"This isn't about me," Henry answered.

"Then butt out," Duncan returned.

"I'm a throwaway, I get that." Henry sighed. "But this is your daughter and grandson."

"They are mine," Duncan agreed.

"You can either shut up and support them, or you can leave right now," Henry asserted.

Duncan saw a lot of Henry's father in him at that moment. For the most part, Duncan found Henry had Grace's more submissive personality. Push comes to shove, he could tap into his father's fire.

"I am doing what is best for them," Duncan argued.

"Like you did when you shipped me off to Peru when I was nine?" Elizabeth rejoined.

"I had my reasons," he replied.

"Yeah, Mom asked for a divorce," she snipped.

"I kept your family together!" Duncan fumed.

"Stop yelling at Mama!" Richard demanded, coming from behind Henry. He grabbed his heaving stomach and covered his mouth with one hand. Try as he might he couldn't fight the burning sensation coming up. The red liquid spouted out of his mouth and spattered all over the floor.

Henry knelt on the floor next to his son. His eyes widened. "That's blood."

"Angel?" Elizabeth rubbed his back.

Richard went limp. She caught him before he collapsed onto the floor.

She watched the color drain from his skin. "Richard!" she screamed.

Elizabeth's doctor looked up from a chart where he sat on the nurses' hub. Within moments he and a team of nurses surrounded the mother and child.

The doctor knelt down on the floor. He brought the stethoscope off his neck and stuck the earpieces in his ears. He listened to Richard's lungs and heart. "Get a transport gurney in here!" he ordered. "Page Dr. Miles!"

Dr. Fritz took Richard into his arms and he lifted him to the gurney. The boy groaned at being laid down but did not open his eyes. "Richard, baby?" Elizabeth coaxed. He lay there so still. Her chest tightened.

They ran along the gurney down to an elevator. A doctor waited for them with a team of nurses.

"What do we have?" the doctor questioned. He began his own assessment of the small figure on the gurney.

"Five-year-old male presented with gastric pain and vomiting," Dr. Fritz recounted. "He passed out two minutes ago."

"How many times has he thrown up?" Dr. Miles put on his stethoscope.

"Multiple times in the past twelve hours," Henry answered.

"Any food intake during that time?" The doctor looked up at the parents as he listened to Richard's stomach.

"We got him to drink some water, but he hasn't eaten anything solid since lunch yesterday," Henry answered.

Dr. Miles frowned.

"He vomited blood right before he collapsed," Henry added.

"What's his name?" Dr. Miles asked.

"Richard," Elizabeth's voiced cracked.

Dr. Miles lifted one of Richard's eyelids up and checked his pupil with a penlight. "Did he hit his head when he collapsed?"

Elizabeth shook her head. "No, I caught him."

"I need him in endoscopy last week," he called to his team.

"Do whatever you have to do. Just, please, save my baby," Elizabeth pleaded.

"You can't come with us," one nurse stopped them as they came to a set of double doors. "The doctor will come and get you."

Henry had to take Elizabeth by the shoulders to hold her back. The doors swung shut between them.

"He's in good hands," Dr. Fritz assured her.

"Babe, breathe," Henry rubbed her shoulders.

"We should get you sitting." Dr. Fritz motioned them toward the waiting area for endoscopy.

They settled on the hard row of chairs. Henry tucked Elizabeth up under his arm as she laid her head on his shoulder. Elizabeth clutched his shirt for dear life.

Henry stared off to nowhere in particular. His blue eyes were haunted, distant. He ordered himself not to cry. If he started to cry, he couldn't be there for Elizabeth.

Duncan watched on as Elizabeth sobbed into Henry.

An hour passed with no word. "When will they let us know what's going on?" Duncan grumbled.

"After they fix what's wrong," Henry ground out.

"Easy for you to say," Duncan muttered.

"I love my boy!" Henry burst. His face contorted from the tears that were on the verge of falling.

"Sleep deprivation and stress are getting to your head," Duncan scolded.

Henry wanted to open his mouth to set Duncan straight. He didn't. There was no energy left in his bones.

RESTORATION

Dr. Miles removed his surgical cap as he walked into the waiting room. He approached Elizabeth. "Ms. Harper?"

Henry helped Elizabeth stand. He kept an arm around her for support.

"How is my son?" she asked.

"Richard is in recovery. They'll move him to ICU shortly," Dr. Miles reported.

"Can we see him?" Elizabeth requested.

"He hasn't come out of the anesthesia just yet," Dr. Miles replied. He motioned for them to sit. "We should talk first." He sat and the rest of them followed suit.

"What's wrong with him?" Henry inquired.

"Richard suffered two perforated ulcers," Dr. Miles reported. Elizabeth covered her mouth with her hand. "I sutured the affected areas," Dr. Miles continued.

"You had to open him up?" Duncan interjected.

"Who are you?" the doctor inquired.

"I'm Duncan Harper, Richard's grandfather."

Dr. Miles caught Elizabeth's eyes. She nodded.

"Luckily, I was able to go in laparoscopically and repair the ulcers," the doctor replied.

"Is he going to be OK?" Elizabeth wiped her eyes.

"As of now, his prognosis is good, but Richard's got a couple more possible lesions that worry me," Dr. Miles answered.

"You mean he could have another?" Elizabeth asked.

"I'll just say returning him to the same environment is asking for another catastrophic incident," the doctor answered.

"That's a major assumption," Duncan remarked.

"A five-year-old child should not have ulcers," the doctor asserted. He leveled a knowing look at Duncan. "And I have read his history," Dr. Miles added. "They both tell me this child is in an exceptionally stressful, probably abusive, environment."

Elizabeth hung her head. Dr. Miles glanced down at the purple marks on Elizabeth. "Is the man that put those bruises around your neck still at home?"

"If he isn't, he'll be coming back." Elizabeth nodded. "I've been trying to get a divorce."

The doctor nodded.

"Is this the result of what happened last night?" Duncan asked.

"Ulcers do not pop up overnight, Mr. Harper," Dr. Miles chided. "This built up over several months."

"If the problem was in his stomach, why did he pass out?" Henry asked.

"If I was a betting man, I'd say he passed out from extreme pain," the doctor replied.

Everyone was silent for a moment. Dr. Miles's pager went off. He checked the message.

"Ms. Harper, if you'll come with me. They have him situated." Dr. Miles rose to his feet.

"Great," Duncan stood.

"ICU has a strict number of visitors to two at one time," the doctor looked between the two men.

"Go home, Dad," Elizabeth instructed.

"Henry gets to go back?" Duncan protested.

"He's not the one who's been combative with the mother."

Dr. Miles put his pager back on his belt.

He led the parents through the hospital corridors using the time to give them more information. "Richard's going to have to stay with us for at least five days," Dr. Miles instructed. "I want to monitor him very closely."

"Whatever he needs," Henry agreed.

"Pneumonia is a big worry. Then the reopening of the ulcers is also a possibility," the doctor added.

"How can we help take care of him?" Elizabeth inquired.

"Help Richard remain calm, comfort him," Dr. Miles answered.

"We can do that," Henry said.

They came upon Richard's room. Elizabeth and Henry went right to his bed. "Angel, Mama's here," she cooed.

"Mama?" Richard groaned.

"I'm right here." Elizabeth brushed his hair out of his face. His blue eyes fluttered open.

"Hey, buddy, I'm Dr. Miles," the doctor greeted. "How are you doing? Are you hurting?"

"A little," Richard answered.

"Can you tell me where?" Dr. Miles asked.

"Tummy sore." Richard's eyes flickered as though they were about to close.

Dr. Miles got out his stethoscope and listened to the child's stomach. "We'll keep an eye on that, OK?" He stood. "I'll let you rest and check in on you later," the doctor excused himself.

"We were so worried about you, little prince," Henry cooed.

"I'm sleepy, Mama." Richard's eyelids had half closed.

"Go back to sleep," Elizabeth coaxed. "Henry and I will be

right here when you wake up."

"Rest," Henry urged.

Richard wrapped his hand around three of Henry's fingers. He closed his eyes. Richard tugged Henry's hand in, tucking it just underneath his chin.

"Lie down," Elizabeth whispered.

"What about you?" Henry queried. The bed wasn't big enough for all three of them.

"I am fine. Our son needs you right now," she insisted.

Elizabeth took her spot on a nearby couch.

At the sound of feet entering the doorway, Henry lifted his head. Oliver nodded to his friend. Miranda entered side by side with her husband. Victoria followed on their heels.

Elizabeth straightened her curled-up legs and sat up. Henry gingerly detangled himself from his son. Richard didn't even stir this time.

Oliver walked over and surveyed the sleeping child. Henry met him. "How is he?" Oliver whispered.

"Weak and exhausted." Henry's shoulders fell.

"He's a fighter," Oliver encouraged.

Victoria kissed Richard's forehead. "We better talk outside." Before the nurses asked them to leave.

Henry joined Elizabeth leaning against the wall while Miranda and Oliver stood opposite them.

"We have enough evidence to file the divorce papers under cruel treatment," Miranda informed them.

"If Dad doesn't decide to block it," Elizabeth muttered.

"I brought copies of the orders of protection for you to read," Miranda announced. "We're still working on trying to find Arthur to have him served."

"Good luck with that. Dad's keeping him from the police." Elizabeth frowned.

"Wouldn't be so sure about that. I sent Steven to help the police arrest the lunatic," Victoria replied.

"I have forms for you to sign to get the passports," Miranda stated. "Henry asked for them. Tristian gave me the photos."

Elizabeth took up the first passport form and read it. Henry's photo and information were all labeled properly, so she set it aside. "Why are there four?" She frowned. Elizabeth looked hers over. Nothing was out of the ordinary, so she went on to Richard's. "This is wrong: his last name is Harper." Elizabeth frowned. "And his middle name isn't Duncan, it's Paris after Henry's."

"Someone went in and filed to have his name changed. His legal name is Richard Corbin," Miranda explained.

"How could I not be notified of that? Wouldn't it cause an issue with the insurance or something?" Elizabeth questioned.

"The reason it hasn't given you any problems with the insurance or hospital is that his social security number is still registered to the name you originally gave him and you have the original birth certificate."

"Arthur, you bastard," Elizabeth grumbled.

"You think he did it?" Miranda questioned.

"If Father had done it, he would have changed the social too," Elizabeth pointed out.

"He'd need both you and Richard in person at the social security office," Miranda pointed out.

"It's not that hard to find stand-ins in this town," Oliver replied.

"If you're going to go through filing to change his name again, it might be best to file with the proper information," Miranda encouraged.

"One battle at a time," Henry replied.

"It'll give you, even more, leverage to terminate Arthur's rights to Richard," Miranda advised.

"If we can prove I'm Richard's father, why would Arthur have any rights?" Henry frowned.

"As Elizabeth's husband at the time of birth, he has some legal standing," Miranda said. "But if we are able to bring in evidence of this attack and then the first one on Richard, any reasonable judge would vacate them."

Elizabeth gasped and put a hand to her chest. "Mom, I am so sorry."

"It's OK, honey, I already know." Victoria squeezed her shoulders.

"Can you help me with a will?" Elizabeth asked.

"Sure," Miranda replied.

"Dad would try to bury it, but I need to have something set up that says Richard goes to Henry," Elizabeth said.

"We need to leave," Henry argued.

"What would you have done if I had—" Elizabeth began.

He cut her off. "Please, Elizabeth, I can't talk about this right now."

"It's something we need to talk about," she insisted.

"I would have grabbed Richard and ran," Henry raked his hand through his hair. "I wouldn't have had any other option."

Elizabeth pressed her lips together. "That's what I'd want

you to do. Richard would need to be with you." Something Duncan would fight tooth and nail.

"He needs to be with us," Henry countered. "Both of us." Elizabeth sniffled. "He needs us to make sure he has the peace to heal," he said, his voice turned pleading.

"Hear, hear," Tristian approached them from down the hall.

"Tristian?" Elizabeth gulped.

"You didn't think I wouldn't come by and check on my favorite model?" the photographer asked.

"Thanks for coming," Henry replied.

"If peace is what you're looking for, Tahiti is one of the most laid back places I've ever been," Tristan said.

Henry's ears perked up. "That's where you wanted to do the shoot, right?"

"I have my own condo there," Tristian offered. "You could stay there for a while."

"That is a very generous offer," Elizabeth began.

"You don't have to do the shoot. I was only pushing to get you out of the mansion and away from Arthur," Tristian said.

"Dad is not going to let me take Richard out of California." Elizabeth shook her head.

"We will get him on that plane." Henry put his hand on Elizabeth's shoulder.

"If Dad finds us, he'll take Richard," Elizabeth protested.

"If we have to move you to a second location, we'll do it," Oliver promised.

"I can't lose my baby," Elizabeth's voice cracked.

"We won't," Henry vowed.

"I should have run with you before the wedding like you begged me to," she said, deflated.

Henry took her face in his hands. "Run away with me now."

Chapter Seventeen

D r. Miles handed off a chart to a nurse when he saw his youngest patient coming down the hall. "Fancy meeting you here," he said and smiled.

Richard waved to his doctor. "'Ello."

"I see you've been walking around like I told you to," Dr. Miles praised.

Richard nodded.

"Your color is better too," the doctor added. "How are you feeling?"

"Better," Richard answered.

"Walk you to your room?" Dr. Miles offered. "How's the eating going?"

"I like applesauce," Richard said.

"Can't get him to touch the Jell-O," Henry snickered.

The doctor laughed. "I don't blame you, Ricky. If it doesn't look or smell good to you, don't eat it," the doctor advised.

Henry motioned him back for a moment. Dr. Miles let Richard and Elizabeth lead.

"Yes, Mr. Angevin," the doctor opened.

"How long until Richard can travel?" Henry inquired.

"What mode of transportation?" Dr. Miles asked.

"Flying," Henry bit his bottom lip.

The doctor read between the lines. "Has he flown before?" Dr. Miles questioned.

"I'm not sure. His mother would know that better than me," Henry answered.

"If it stresses him, don't do it," the doctor advised. "Under normal circumstances, I wouldn't recommend it for a while, but if Richard seems OK with the idea, he's cleared after he's discharged today."

Henry's shoulders relaxed.

"He'll need to remain in the care of a physician for the next few months at least," Dr. Miles cautioned.

Henry nodded. "That's one of the first things we'll be looking into when we get there."

"Here's your stop," Dr. Miles said when they got to Richard's room.

"I'll go get the ball rolling on Richard's discharge paperwork."

Richard frowned at the statement.

"What's the matter?" Henry asked.

"Are we going to have to go back to Grandad's?" Richard asked.

"No," Henry stated.

Elizabeth sat down and brought Richard onto her lap. She locked eyes with him. "We're going to take a trip," Elizabeth informed her son.

"A trip? W'ere we go?" the little boy asked.

"You remember Tristian asked Mama to go to an island to take pictures?" she reminded him.

"We're going to an island?" Richard marveled.

Elizabeth nodded her head. "You, me, and Henry are going to get on a big plane."

"Really?" Hs eyes brightened at the thought.

"Sounds fun. Right, little prince?" Henry grinned.

Richard nodded brightly.

Oliver got out and helped get their luggage out of the trunk. "You're going to have to buy some things when you get there," he noted. The bags were rather light. "Are you sure you don't want me to wait with you?" Oliver asked.

"No, you should get back home to your wife and kids." Henry reached out and hugged his friend. Oliver returned the embrace. "Thanks for everything." Henry's eyes misted.

"Come on, man, this isn't goodbye forever," Oliver assured him. "I'm bringing the family down to visit soon."

"You better," Henry said.

"We'll be expecting you guys in Aspen for Christmas." Oliver patted him on the back.

"I'll write it on the calendar," Henry replied.

"See ya, buddy." He waved to Richard before getting back in his car and driving off.

Bags checked, they made their way through security. The gate for their plane wasn't too far off.

Richard walked between them holding their hands. When Duncan stood from a nearby section of chairs, Elizabeth's heart sank.

"I'll go talk to him." Henry set a backpack down to claim a chair.

"No, stay with Ricky," Elizabeth urged. "If anything goes sideways, get Ricky on that plane."

She crossed to her father.

"Relax, it's just me, Lizzie." Duncan held out his arms in a show of vulnerability.

"How did you know we were here?" she asked.

"I'm not stupid," he said through a half smile.

"That is one thing you are not," Elizabeth agreed.

"Did you think you could go and not let me say goodbye?" Duncan questioned.

"Are you going to try to stop us?" Elizabeth dropped her shoulders.

"I should," he said.

"But?"

"You're desperate to get Richard healing," Duncan acknowledged.

"I've got to protect my baby," she insisted.

"The best solution is to rip him from his home and take him somewhere he's never been?" he queried.

"Dad, don't." Elizabeth lifted her hand. She glanced back through the door to see Henry sitting with Richard on his lap.

Duncan inhaled. "Henry is good with Richard as much as it pains me to say it."

"This isn't about taking him away from you, OK? It's about making sure he sees his sixth birthday," Elizabeth asserted.

"If you really wanted to disappear, you would have at the very least used different names on the passports," Duncan reasoned. "Something tells me you still don't want to completely cut ties with me."

"I miss the dad you were when I was seven," Elizabeth

lamented.

"Do you have a house? What are you going to do?" he inquired.

"Tristian is letting us stay in his place while we look for something," she replied.

"Do I get to know where you are staying after that?" Duncan asked.

"I'll talk it over with Henry. Remember: if I'm in Tahiti, I can't be here to press charges against Arthur," she proposed.

"Can I say goodbye to my grandson?" he requested. Elizabeth led him over.

"Truce. I come in peace," Duncan said. Henry eyed him warily. Duncan knelt on one knee. "Mama said you guys are going on a trip." He addressed his grandson.

"We're gonna fly in an airplane," Richard announced.

He kissed Richard's forehead. "I am going to miss you so much." His voice genuinely cracked. He embraced Richard.

The boarding call was announced over the speaker.

Duncan got to his feet as did Henry.

"You can come down to visit, but if Arthur makes it down to Tahiti, he's not coming back," Henry leveled. Duncan nodded and let them walk away.

The little family headed for the plane.

———

Eyes closed, Elizabeth inhaled deeply relishing the smell of salt water. She opened her eyes. Off the balcony, she had a clear view of the sea. The crystal teal of the ocean made her smile.

Henry caught Elizabeth by her waist. He guided her back

to him. She sighed contentedly as Henry kissed her temple. There were worse places to be confined to.

"Beautiful, isn't it?" She melted back into him.

"Your smile is beautiful." Henry smirked.

Elizabeth laughed. "Shut up."

"You're amazing," he marveled.

"Did you get the doctor's appointment for Richard?" she inquired.

"9:00 a.m. tomorrow," Henry informed her. "We got a call from the real estate agent. He said there is another condo on the next floor up for sale."

"I think it might be worth looking into." Elizabeth pursed her lips. "Unless you want a house."

He shrugged. "Either is fine."

"You can have a preference," she encouraged.

"I don't think I have one. I mean I've really only lived in apartments, but I don't have anything against a house," Henry said.

"I want you to be happy with where we live too," Elizabeth insisted.

"As long as you and Richard are happy"—Henry paused to kiss her—"I am happy."

"Oh, you're no help," she teased.

"Maybe we should ask Richard," Henry suggested. He eased himself down to sit on the foot of the lounge chair where Richard reclined. "What do you think? Do you like Tristian's condo?" Henry asked.

"I do." Richard nodded. "It's nice here. Can we go to the beach?" he requested.

"I don't see why not," Henry agreed.

"You'll have to tell us when you get tired," Elizabeth

instructed.

"OK," Richard agreed.

Henry gathered up supplies while Elizabeth applied sunscreen to Richard.

They found a great spot not too far from the water.

"How about we go build some sand castles?" Henry held up the bucket. "Let's fill it up." He gave Richard a toy shovel. They both dug up some sea-moistened sand. "Pat it tight," Henry directed. They patted the sand in tight.

Henry lifted the bucket leaving a column of damp sand standing.

"Time to carve." Henry gave Richard a small twig. With another he showed Richard how to mark in doors and windows in the sand.

Elizabeth leaned back on her elbow, watching her guys play in the sand. She was going to enjoy this respite for as long as it lasted.

Other Titles by Sonja Gambrell

Richard Angevin is a survivor. Growing up the scion of a Hollywood powerhouse family is not as glamorous as it sounds. Behind closed doors is another story. He refuses to let the abuse he suffered in childhood make him hard. Life finally seems to be going his way. Now grown and an actor, he is married to the love of his life, Ophelia. Their infant son, Henry, is the icing on the cake. The peace Richard has found is torn to shambles when Ophelia and Henry are kidnapped by a jealous ex-tormentor. While Ophelia struggles to keep Henry and herself alive, Richard has to face the demons from his past as he fights to get his family back. Will they be reunited? Or will his bloodstained heart completely shatter?

About the Author

Sonja Gambrell has a passion for writing which began at age four, when she dictated her stories to her mother. While growing up in a military family, Sonja and her three sisters were home schooled by their mother. Sonja graduated with honors from Campbell University. Sonja enjoys writing, theatre, music appreciation, oil painting, and spending time with her six nieces and three nephews. She currently resides in North Carolina.